The Author

MORLEY CALLAGHAN was born in Toronto, Ontario, in 1903. A graduate of the University of Toronto and Osgoode Law School, he was called to the bar in 1928, the same year that his first novel, *Strange Fugitive,* was published. Fiction commanded his attention, and he never practised law.

While in university, Callaghan had taken a summer position at the *Toronto Star* when Ernest Hemingway was a reporter there. In April 1929, he travelled with his wife to Paris, where their literary circle of friends included Hemingway, Fitzgerald, and Joyce. *That Summer in Paris* is his memoir of the time. The following autumn, Callaghan returned to Toronto.

Callaghan was among the first writers in Canada to earn his livelihood exclusively from writing. In a career that spanned more than six decades, he published sixteen novels and more than a hundred shorter works of fiction. Usually set in the modern city, his fiction captures the drama of ordinary lives as people struggle against a background of often hostile social forces.

Morley Callaghan died in Toronto, Ontario, in 1990.

THE NEW CANADIAN LIBRARY

General Editor: David Staines

Morley Callaghan

MORE JOY
IN HEAVEN

With an Afterword by Margaret Avison

M&S

First published in 1937 by Random House, New York
Copyright © 1992 by the Estate of Morley Callaghan
Afterword copyright © 1992 by Margaret Avison

New Canadian Library edition 1992

Canadian Cataloguing in Publication Data

Callaghan, Morley, 1903-1990
More joy in heaven

(New Canadian library)
ISBN 0-7710-9956-8

I. Title. II. Series

PS8505.A5M6 1992   C813'.52   C89-093677-3
PR9199.3.C35M6 1992

We acknowledge the financial support of the Government of Canada through
the Book Publishing Industry Development Program for our publishing
activities. We further acknowledge the support of the Canada Council for the
Arts and the Ontario Arts Council for our publishing program.

The characters and situations in this novel are entirely fictional, and
do not represent or portray any actual persons or events.

Typesetting by M&S, Toronto
Printed and bound in Canada

McClelland & Stewart Ltd.
The Canadian Publishers
481 University Avenue
Toronto, Ontario
M5G 2E9
www.mcclelland.com

3 4 5   03 02 01 00

One

SENATOR Maclean, the investment banker and mining magnate, watched at the window for hours for the car to come down the road from the prison. His white hair was ruffled, his clothes were creased and his pink face looked very tired. He had been trying to sleep, but he kept going back to the window. In the dawn light, with the wind driving the hard snow against the panes, he could see nothing but the shapes of the houses along the village road, and his snow-covered car under the hotel light.

Along that road beyond the town was the prison in the hills. The country seemed to rise up all around him in the snow, dawn light and loneliness. Feeling exhausted, he asked himself what he was doing there on Christmas morning waiting for a convict when he should be at home in the city in his warm bed. This whole thing could ruin him. "Am I just showing off, waiting like this for Caley?" he asked himself, knowing he had a weakness for making showy gestures to the nation and that people like Judge Ford who disliked him called him a reckless exhibitionist, a man of irresponsible generosity. As a final test he asked himself, "What's there in it for me?" He knew the answer was "Nothing at all." He was relieved; he was only following his intuition for doing the thing that touched the inarticulate aspiration of millions of people.

Suddenly he heard the car coming down the road. He grabbed his hat and his big coonskin coat and hurried down the creaking stairs to the dimly lit lobby, and watched the door with its Christmas wreath and red paper bell. The door opened, but it was only the big, raw-boned, sandy-haired prison chaplain coming in alone and pulling his gloves off.

"Did you bring him, Father?" he called.

"I didn't think you'd be awake."

"You didn't bring him?"

"I'll have him here in twenty minutes," he said. Everybody in the hotel was asleep and their voices sounded loud; so the priest came to the foot of the stairs.

"You didn't need to wake me. I haven't slept for hours," the Senator said.

"Are you worried?"

"No, no, no – I'm just a little excited. Look, before you go, how about a drink? It'll warm us both up."

The priest shook his head apologetically. "I don't like going down there with the smell of liquor on my breath," he said. "It's not that I don't take it."

"Come on, I'll give you a big black cigar to hide it," said the Senator, and though he was only offering a little thing it made him feel opulent and sure of himself.

"Of course, it being Christmas ..."

"Why, sure, Merry Christmas, that's right!" the Senator said, and he slipped his arm under the priest's. They went up to his room. As he poured the whiskey he watched the priest moving around the room restlessly.

"Sit down, sit down," he said, and the priest sat down on the bed. They smiled at each other, both feeling how strange it was that they should be there at dawn together. "Take your time, a few minutes won't matter," the Senator said. As the priest leaned closer to him the Senator felt his eagerness being restored; he felt he was suddenly seeing the priest as Caley saw him and he wondered what it was in the man that was so deep

and gentle and strong. He was no plaster saint. Many people of
his own faith didn't like him. Bishop Murray, who often mort-
gaged church property to the Senator, found the priest irasci-
ble and grim. Sometimes his breath smelled of whiskey and he
was apt to fly into a temper and then sigh and speak out of the
deepest charity. He had walked to the gallows with sixteen
men, and everybody in the prison marvelled that none of
them had died badly. But it had brought him some kind of
fever and he broke out into nervous sweats and had to change
his underwear three or four times a day. The Senator wanted
to hold him there and share his concern with him.

"I couldn't sleep. I got thinking of the first time I ever saw
Caley – that day he stood up in the dock ten years ago," he said.
"I can still see him getting up slowly and his mother and kid
brother holding on to each other, scared, and us all terribly
excited. Then he started to shout at Judge Ford, trying to tell
him why he turned bank robber. You should have been there.
The words poured out of him – they couldn't stop him. They
grabbed at him like little dogs at the throat of a big black bull.
And all he was trying to tell us was that he had always been different and made his own rules."

"And he certainly was different then," the priest said.

"Yet it's all gone – that's the wonderful thing – with your
help."

"Not me! I had nothing to do with it. Getting close to other
men and getting out of himself did it."

"I mean his big special feeling's gone."

"It's turned into something else."

"I was thinking about it, lying there. Why, it's like a bit of
magic. A few years ago you'd have sworn he never could have
got rid of it."

"A prison is full of big special characters," the priest said.

"Not like him. You'll never get another one like him."

"Maybe no one as intelligent. When they began to look like
freaks to him he wanted to be normal, that's all."

"Nothing seems normal at dawn," the Senator said. "Everything looms up bigger." He wanted to tell how worried he had been, waiting at the window, but he said, "I'm not religious like you. I've spent most of my life making money and tossing it around carelessly and the only thing I can get out of this is a lot of abuse from people, but it's given me a big lift, a strange kind of a buggy ride."

"Ah, Senator, if I had a parish made up of all the people you've helped I'd have to build a great church to hold them."

"A few dollars here, a few there…. Giving a man a dollar isn't helping him."

"It's a sign of something."

"Maybe just a way of getting rid of him."

"Not you, Senator," he said. He began tapping his lips with the edge of his glass and seemed to be troubled. "Maybe I'm worrying myself foolishly," he said, but he still pondered. "The trouble is there's probably more public curiosity about him since he became a good man than there was when he was a notorious bank robber, and it worries me."

"Oh, that's just the newspapers. We'll dodge them. It'll all die down."

"I hope so," the priest said as he got up. "He's got a lot of pride and I hope people respect it, that's all." He held the door knob and was still bothered. "He's going with you – but he's paroled in my care. Maybe he should stay with me," he said. And then he smiled, "Of course, he'd want to go to the city and see his mother anyway, wouldn't he?" Going down the stairs he said, "I'll whisk him out and have him here in twenty minutes," and then he was gone.

The Senator couldn't bear to go back to the room; he looked around the lobby as if he never expected to see the hotel again. "I can hear what General Crighton would say if he saw me here," he thought. "Well, to hell with General Crighton." He went out and walked up and down the road in front of the hotel. The snow blew against his hat and he grabbed it and pushed it down hard over his white head. He wiped his pink cheeks, and ducked his chin down in the collar of his big fur coat. It was a little lighter now but the hills beyond the town were still shadowy humps against the sky.

His feet crunched on the snow and he began to worry again. The priest was right. Too many people had talked about Caley. Every political committee investigating penitentiary conditions had asked to see the famous bank robber, marvelled at his new peacefulness and dignity, and had told their stories to the papers. Yet the Senator knew that if it hadn't been for these stories he himself might never have got interested in Caley.

Behind the cold hills a line of light was rising, making them glint like crystals. While he watched the line of light he saw the car coming down the road. As the car stopped on the side the priest got out; and then Caley came towering up wide-shouldered behind him, huger than ever in that wintry half light. The Senator tried anxiously to catch a glimpse of his face, wondering if in that light he wouldn't still look like that big dark wild-eyed violent criminal he had heard shouting at the Judge ten years ago.

Caley had his hat off. The wind was blowing in his black hair. He came across the road leaning against the wind, turning his dark high-cheekboned face so the snow would sting it. Then he called, "Hello, Senator," and he was closer; you could see his face and he was laughing.

Feeling in Caley that same deep, peaceful confidence he felt all those times he had talked with him in prison about little and big things the Senator was deeply moved. "Hello, Kip," he called eagerly.

"Gee, Senator," Caley said, grabbing his hand, "what can a guy say?" His vitality and eagerness seemed to break over the Senator in a flow of jerky words. "It's the most beautiful morning in all history."

Snow was melting on Caley's face as he looked along the

street and up at the sky. The Senator took his arm and walked him along to the car. "Let's get out of here before anyone sees us," he said. While he was getting in, the priest and Caley stood together in the snow, just looking at each other, gripping hands.

They had been together ten years and now, parting, they were trying to say something adequate to the good memory. "Good luck, son," said the priest.

And Kip hardly whispered, "We've been together a long time. We got hold of something between us – it's still between us, we can't break it, being away from each other, see?"

"It's all right if we keep thinking of each other. I'll pray for you," the priest replied.

Then Kip got into the car. When they looked back they saw the priest standing alone in the highway looking after them, and the wind had already blown the snow over the footprints of Kip and the priest on the road.

"He's a most remarkable man," the Senator said.

"He's bigger than you or me or any of us. He's made me feel like a plugged nickel from the time I first met him. He's got the same feeling for everybody."

"It's true," said the Senator. "I know how you feel."

"I'm a little excited, I guess," he laughed.

"Why shouldn't you be? I am too," the Senator said.

Riding along through the snow with the big eager man beside him, the Senator thought, "It's like handing him a new life." He felt within himself great power and exultation. He felt like a creator. He tried to keep it simple and secret by talking about little things. He wanted Kip to take a job with Jenkins at the Coronet Hotel. He told him some broker friends had taken up a collection of a hundred dollars to help him along. In the morning he wanted him to go to his tailor and order some good suits.

"That's all swell," Kip said. "Gee, Senator, I'd like to lose myself like a kid in a big city. I never want them to find me.

That's my idea of what would be pretty swell – going on from day to day lost in a town you're crazy about, bumping into something fresh every day, finding out how it all worked in together."

The sound of his eager voice expressing such a humble wish for a kind of life he had never lived exalted the Senator. Kip was talking about milkmen driving their wagons along the street at dawn, of janitors taking out garbage, of old men sitting gossiping on verandas at twilight, of walking along the street in the spring watching the girls in their new Easter clothes. Then he sat up stiff and said, "Stop the car, Senator."

"What's the matter?"

"That field over there."

There were no woods around for miles, just snow-covered rolling fields with a slope leading up to a farmhouse far back on the hill. There were lights in the windows of the farmhouse, which looked dreadfully lonely in the fields of snow. Up in the barn a rooster began to crow, a door slammed, a farmer came out of the house with a pail in his hand and walked toward the barn.

"That's the field," Kip said. "I wondered if I'd be able to pick it out; that's it, all right."

"What is it?"

"You remember the time I told Judge Ford I'd escape?"

"Yes."

"That's the field we hid in. Joe Foley and me, only it was raining and it was about this time in the morning. There was a big pile of hay over there and we hid in the hay all day and the farmer didn't touch it because it was wet. A dog stuck his nose in and started to bark and I hauled it in and choked it with my hands. Just a minute," he said. He got out, and went up on the bank at the side of the road and stood looking across the field at the farmhouse. When he turned around, his dark excited face full of the memory of that field, he loomed up huge against the dawn skyline.

Two

T HEY DROVE all day and it was night when they got to —— on the lake. When they came to the bridge leading to the neighborhood where Kip was born he begged the Senator to leave him. He wanted to go on alone to his mother's house. He walked through the snow half way over the bridge and his stride was so long the footprints he left in the fresh snow were like the marks from the stride of a man who had been running. Half way over the bridge he stopped and took off his hat and let the snowflakes make little white melting patterns in his thick black hair. He was looking down at the ice on the river as he used to do when he was a kid – at the lines of railroad tracks curving down to the bay, the snow-capped box cars row on row, and the old metal plant, dark and silent on Christmas night. Beyond were the points of light in the houses of the poor homes in the neighborhood.

But it seemed to him that he was crossing the bridge into a new country that he discovered after many lonely hours in his cell, wondering what had happened to his life. In prison there had been order and solitude for him instead of reckless violence. He had had a lot of quiet time. There was no chance for excitement. He had been truly alone with himself for the first time in his life then. Now he could ask himself what had happened to him that his life was over. Something seemed to have gone wrong for him somewhere. He felt like a big kid with clumsy fingers trying to take a watch to pieces to find out why it had stopped ticking. Bits of his life were scattered in his memory; he wanted to stretch them out together and look at them. When he was a kid his mother and younger brother, Denis, and his dead sister, Nellie, seemed to be afraid of him. His father had deserted him; he couldn't remember him. Other kids used to follow him around waiting for him to lead them to things they were afraid to touch. He stole a bicycle when he was nine. He had odd jobs, he loafed in the pool parlors, he was often in the juvenile courts, and he learned that everybody, the big and the little, tried to get as much as they could for themselves. But the way they did it seemed dull and unexciting. He was going around like a fire horse waiting for the sound of the bell. Bank robbing came easy and it gave him everything he wanted, direct action, money, excitement, women, a rush across the country with his fame following, and the newspapers full of his pictures and stories celebrating his audacity and courage. Looking back at it, he used to say to himself in the prison, "I must have jumped the tracks somewhere – look what it added up to." If it was the end, then everything had to be re-evaluated with this end in his mind. And as he went back over his life night after night, he made little discoveries that stirred him. "I guess I was always playing myself against the field, making my own rules. I never wanted to work with anybody – that's where I jumped the tracks," he said to himself. "I thought I was too big a guy." Though he was in prison, he could at least make peace with himself. He began to look around at the other convicts, wondering why they were there, feeling that they were his comrades. When he was with his friend the prison chaplain, Father Butler, they talked as if they were two comrades on some kind of journey. He worked with the convicts; he worked with the warden and the guards. Everybody began to trust him. In joining himself with his comrades and the guards, he seemed to join himself to life.

He felt peaceful and almost free. And people began to come from far off to see him.

He walked slowly across the bridge, and at the corner of the narrow street where his mother lived he passed two kids about ten years old, who were leaning against the corner lamp-post. The kid in the leather jacket caught up to him and walked beside him without speaking, his mouth hanging open. At the next street-light Kip turned suddenly; the kid's eyes were crazy with excitement. Snatching off his hat the kid whispered, "Aren't you Uncle Kip?"

"Uncle Kip?"

"Yeah, my Uncle Kip."

"I don't know you, son."

"I mean," the kid said, stopping short as if his breath was cut off, "you're Kip Caley, aren't you?"

"You said it, son."

"Well – well – you're my uncle – that's all," he said, looking up at him with a kind of trembling wonder. "Gee whiz," he said. Clutching his hat tight in his hand he ran down the street lurching and spinning on the icy sidewalk, and darted through the crowd gathered in front of the house.

When Kip got to that narrow red brick house, one house under a long roof running the length of the street, someone yelled. A couple of women came out across the street with coats thrown loosely around their shoulders.

"Hey, Kip, wait a minute, just a minute before you go in," a man with a camera yelled. "Stand just where you are – there."

While Kip looked around helplessly at the gathering crowd they started taking flashlight pictures of him. They scared him. Once he turned, as if to run away. Someone had hold of him by the arm. In the falling snow faces seemed to come leaping out at him wet and shining – faces he didn't know till he saw the kid in the leather jacket.

Dazed, he tried to smile. Waving his hand, he shouted, "Merry Christmas to the bunch of you!"

"Same to you, Kip," they yelled.

"Just stand there, Kip," the newspaperman yelled, and the flashlights kept popping.

"What is this?" he said

"Your birthday."

"Like hell," he said, and he waved his hand, pushed them out of his path and ran up to the door in the red brick house and pushed it open.

Leaning all his weight against the door he bolted it, muttering, "They're not coming in." His face showed such desolation that his mother and brother, standing at the end of a table heaped with food in the little living room, took a few hesitant steps toward him. His mother was a little plump woman with a kind of fearful quietness in her, with blue eyes like a frightened girl's eyes. His brother, Denis, who had none of his own great height and broad shoulders, was slim and serious, a young doctor turning prematurely bald, who looked as if he had exhausted himself for twenty years working his way through medicine and trying to free himself from Kip's life.

"Kip," Denis whispered, "Kip," almost scared to move toward him and touch him. The mother didn't move either for a moment. Her lower jaw began to tremble, the loose skin on her throat seemed to contract and loosen and she began to cry quietly.

But he was listening to the pounding on the door, a steady, eager pounding, and the sound of excited voices. When he turned to his mother and brother he shook his big head and looked sick with disappointment.

"What do they want?" he said. "I wanted to come here alone. I didn't think they'd notice me. I didn't think they'd remember me."

"They've been here all day," his mother whispered.

"Who?"

"Newspapermen, people on the streets."

"People from all over," Denis said bitterly.

While the pounding grew louder and the voices rose, Kip whispered helplessly, "Aren't they going to give me a chance? Ten years is a long time. Ten years I've been away and they don't know me. Ten years and the people we knew on the street must be all gone. What are they doing there?"

"Ah, they're going to give you a chance, son. Such a chance they want to give you," his mother said.

"They don't forget you," Denis said.

"Me?"

"They haven't forgotten you."

"But I'm – well, just nobody right now," he said. Listening, he backed away from the door, frightened. He put one of his big arms around his mother and drew her head against his shoulder and let her sob. The feeling of her sobbing there close to him gave him the delight of a child. He said, "Ten years, mom – ten years is pretty long, but look how it passed. It wasn't for life. Look how it passed. Look how it worked out, and here we are." He wouldn't let her lift her head. His voice was full of gentleness and immense gratification, as if these few moments in this simple relationship with his mother was the beautiful beginning of his new life.

But he felt her trembling and he looked down at her face, surprised. "Are you afraid of me, Mother?"

"No, son, just a little excited."

"You afraid of me, Denis?" he said to his brother, who had never stopped staring at him.

"I was never afraid of you," Denis said.

"I mean do the both of you believe in me? Look, everybody down there believed in me. Why, listen, you do, don't you?" He swung from one to the other, pleading, "Why do you think Senator Maclean was willing to do so much for me? He spent hours with me, days with me. Denis, Mother, I know how you feel. I got a chance to read, I got a chance to think. You know why you pull away from me like that? I come in here and everything seems strange and different to you." He tried to laugh, he stopped and stared at her. "You're right, you don't know me. That's fine. You'll get to know me."

But his mother, with her apron up to her face, wept a little, and said, "Maybe it's the grace and goodness of Almighty God, and oh, son, if it is I'm ashamed because it came at a time when I'd stopped praying because I got used to you like you were."

The pounding at the door and angry shouting kept on, but the mother and the two brothers no longer seemed to hear it. Denis said to Kip, "There's something I got to tell you now because maybe you'll be noticing it later on. I've changed my name. I'm a doctor as you know. But I went all through the medical school under the name of Ritchie, Denis Ritchie. You know why." He faltered, as if he despised himself for a lack of loyalty; but loyalty to Kip had broken his heart for years. With the precision of a cool professional man, he went on doggedly, "I couldn't go into a university with the same name as you. I kept it up all the time I was a kid. They called me the bank robber's brother till I couldn't stand it. They used to say: 'That's Kip Caley's brother.' I got to hate the whole set-up. I wanted you to know right at the start why it was I changed my name."

"Jesus, Denis, you did just what I wanted you to do," Kip said, and he put his arms around his brother's shoulder. "I didn't used to think of you at all – you were just a punk. But in those last few years I've been wondering how it was shaping up for you. It's swell – geez, I'm delighted."

His magnanimous good-will began to overawe them as it used to do when he was a kid, and he laughed and asked, "What name did you pick, Denis?"

"Ritchie – Denis Ritchie."

"That's a hell of a name," he kidded him.

"I just wanted to tell you in case any of those people out there mention it," Denis said. "I'm going to let them in now or they'll be pounding all night."

But Kip grabbed his arm. "Don't let them in, see?" he begged. "I don't want anybody to pay any attention to me. Tell them to go home. Let them pound all night. Please, Denis." Then he stopped and sighed, full of sadness, and he whispered, "Why can't they leave me alone? They're going to give me a ride. They'll have the cops around here. They'll laugh and make a big joke." Looking at the door wildly he muttered, "They're not going to give me a chance. They're going to make it tough and try and run me out of here." At the front door the pounding started all over again. "Go ahead, let them talk to me – we'll get it over," he whispered.

"They haven't been near us for ten years and now they're back again," Denis said.

"Oh, my God!" his mother moaned.

This cry from his mother made him feel ashamed. He wanted suddenly to meet people with such dignity and simplicity that they would leave the house and never bother his mother and brother again.

But a noise in the kitchen made him wheel around, listening to the sound of cautious footsteps. The kitchen door opened slowly. The freckled face of the ten-year-old boy with the long straight hair came slowly in sight, his face white with excitement and his blue eyes in a wild fixed stare. When he saw Kip staring at him, he whispered: "Can I come in, Uncle Kip?"

"Who's the kid?" Kip asked.

"Your sister's boy, Tim."

"Tim, Nellie's boy, Tim, eh? Why, he was just a little shaver, just four years old last time I saw him." Kip put out his hand eagerly. Keeping a few paces back Tim looked up at his big dark face.

"Won't you shake hands, son?" Kip said, feeling the boy ought to hate him because his mother had died broken hearted over him.

"Sure, Uncle Kip," the boy said. But Kip's fumbling tenderness puzzled him.

"You're glad to see me, eh, son?" Kip said.

"I'll tell the world."

"What can I do for you?"

"Just a little thing," said Tim, nervously.

"Go ahead."

"Can a couple of kids come in for a minute?"

"Why, sure, son."

"Gee, that's swell," Tim said. He pushed open the kitchen door and they heard him whisper hoarsely, "Come on, it's all right." Four kids his own age who were waiting and listening in the kitchen – kids in sweaters, woollen hats, old leather jackets, but all with young, pop-eyed faces, came sneaking in and tried to press back against the wall and hide themselves. Tim stood at the door like a policeman, touching each one on the arm as they filed past him. When a lanky, red-headed kid with furtive eyes tried to sneak past he pushed him back heavily and said, "No, you don't, Sambo – I didn't promise it to you."

"Aw geez, Tim, I didn't do nothing to you."

"You had it coming to you and you can't come in," Tim said flatly. The lanky boy was pleading pathetically in the kitchen. But Tim closed the door. Swaggering a little, his face shining with pride, he said to his hand-picked pals, "This is my Uncle Kip."

They stared at Kip's heavy legs and his great shoulders. They were awed. The sight of these children wetting their lips and waiting with their shining eyes began to fill Kip with dread of the city.

"Hey, kids," he said, "I want to shake hands with you. We're going to get to like each other." They beamed at him while he shook hands. "I'm glad to meet you, Mr. Caley." "Gee, Mr. Caley." "Thanks, Mr. Caley." "We heard a lot about you from Tim, Mr. Caley," they said one after another.

Then Kip said to his brother, "Let that bunch out there in. My God, man, why don't you smile?"

"I'm not going to stay here," Denis said. "I'll go upstairs. I don't want to have anything to do with this."

"Go on then," Kip said. "You're kind of sour-faced, but you're swell." And Denis went upstairs.

The frightened kids were still holding themselves tight against the wall. Kip smiled at them. They started to laugh. They moved their legs and scraped their feet in a fine relaxation and began to cough and even look eagerly at Tim who was helping himself to a little cold white chicken meat from the big platter on the table.

"Let them in, Mother," Kip said.

"God help us. They'll have the door down if I don't."

A gust of cold air swept along the hall. He heard the sound of men stamping snow from their feet, then the door was slammed and Mrs. Caley led three newspapermen into the sitting room. One was so thin he looked like a prop for his clothes, with a head that looked like a skull. Another one was very scholarly and detached, with high narrow forehead and thin fair hair, and there was a little short jolly man with long moustaches and laughter lines thick around his eyes. They had evidently agreed to let Smiley, the thin wisp of a man, start the conversation. "How are you doing, Kip? Remember me?" he said easily, his hand out.

"We're respectable people," Kip's mother said to them in a soft begging tone. "I've worked hard all my life. We've had a hard time getting along. We don't want anything from anybody. We're happy, but you'll put our pictures in the paper and try to start everything all over again. Get out, go on. Please, please, leave us alone."

"Ah, don't take it so hard," Kip said to her, as she clenched her hands in her lap grimly.

"Don't you remember me, Kip?" Smiley from the *News* was asking, and he waited humbly, like one of the kids.

"Maybe the old memory isn't what it was," Kip said.

"Maybe I'm slipping. Maybe it's because I've got used to seeing just the same faces the last ten years."

"Listen, think of a train," Smiley said, eagerly.

"It's coming now, go on."

"Think of a train about ten years ago."

"Maybe you've changed a lot."

"No, I weigh just the same. I've got all my hair and all my teeth. Think of having a meal on the train. Think of having a meal and talking a lot," he urged.

"Ten years ago, you say?"

"Yeah, think of a bottle of catsup, me moving it around on the table and then you taking the bottle of catsup and moving it around on the cloth while you looked out the window."

"The train from St. Paul," Kip said, eagerly.

"That's it. St. Paul where they caught you."

"Why, you're Smiley – that swell story, the only guy that gave me a break."

"It was nothing, Kip," Smiley said, and he turned to his friends with his bright little grin. "See, didn't I tell ya? I knew he'd remember me. Why shouldn't I remember him? I got into a terrible jam on the paper when the story came out on account of everybody saying I made a hero of him. I couldn't help it. I got to like the guy." He introduced his two friends. The scholarly one was J.C. Higgins; the plump pudding-faced jolly one with the bunch of wrinkles around his eyes was Tony Billings.

"By God, Kip, you were born to be a headline," Smiley said, snickering to himself as he helped himself to a snack from the table.

"A bigger headline now than you ever were," Tony Billings said.

"Look, you guys," he said anxiously. "Do something for me, will you? Play this down. Give me a break. It's going to be tough for me if you drag all the old stuff out. Please, boys."

"Look at it from our angle, Kip," the plump one said. "The worst man in the world becomes the best man in the world. See what we mean? Give us something from the inside. What is it you'd like to do?"

"Senator Maclean's got a job for me."

"We mean what are you after?" Smiley said.

They were watching his eyes as if he might make some little slip that would betray him, but he said quietly, "I want to be a good man, to fit into things, to live in my own city, and to get a little closer to people than I ever was, and – and – well – just be a pretty good man."

"Good?"

"You say good?"

"What's he getting at?"

Putting both his big rough hands flat on the table he looked right at them, then he turned to the kids. "Better go home, kids," he said. He watched them file out unhappily. "See you again, Tim," he called.

"Here's the way it is, take it or leave it," he said. "I went down there ten years ago and I felt like a chump on account of I got caught and I only wanted to get out and get started again. The only thing that was good in those days was the thing that was good for me, see – that meant the thing I wanted, and that meant money and everything that came with it. I liked the headlines – there wasn't a bank in the country I couldn't open like you'd open a can of tomatoes. I felt bigger than you, or my own people, or the cop on the beat. That made me feel pretty special, see, sort of different. I sort of liked being different – a big guy and different, see. I thought I could be damn near everything I wanted doing it the soft way. I had big crazy ideas, but I took me apart and found out about what makes a guy tick."

His eyes lightened and he smiled. "Remember the old clowns in the burlesque shows? Remember Bozo Snyder and Sliding Billie Watson?" he asked them. "They were so different you thought they were good comics, eh? That was on a stage, see. What comics they'd make out on the streets! Supposing they didn't know they were clowns, and then discovered it." He was trying to make it plain how he wanted to become an ordinary man. "There was a big buck nigger we called Steve down there, and he certainly was different. His brain was softening, see, he was a hop head, and his mind was breaking into little pieces, and he certainly was a pretty special case only more so from day to day. All I mean is I don't want to play ball in that league. I'm for being just like you and your brother and the guy next door, see."

"A beautiful conversion," Tony said, sneering.

"I don't give a damn what you call it. It took," he said.

"Sounds so plausible, eh?" Tony said.

"He's an awfully plausible guy."

"You're smooth, Kip."

"Here I —" In the middle of the sentence he was cut off by the sudden mournful hooting of an engine passing on the tracks that curved under the bridge and along by the lake, and he stopped suddenly and listened, looking all around the room at their faces. The engine hooted again; they heard the rattle and swing of the cars. Tense, he whispered, "Think of a train, eh! That's what you said, isn't it, Smiley? There she goes. There she goes skirting the lake. Where's she coming from?" The pain of remembering was in his eyes. "It seemed funny hearing it, sitting here like this," he said softly. "I guess it was you mentioning that train up from St. Paul, Smiley." He was full of the memory of a hundred trains, riding the rods bound west, his face cut to pieces with the cinders, the big meals in the club cars with the boys on that big spending trip to New York; his hands handcuffed to the detective, that trip down to the penitentiary; the everlasting night that first year lying awake in the cell and listening for the sound of the freight train, the wheels gathering speed, the swinging through the dark. Slowly he stood up, and said huskily, "Maybe that's all, eh, gentlemen? I'm tired, terribly tired. How about giving me a break?"

His mother, who had kept on staring at them sullenly, blurted out, "Leave him alone!" Then she started to cry, her head down, and when she looked up her face showed all the misery she must have felt remembering her own fears as he told of the change in him. "We're tired now. Please," she begged them.

But there were still a few questions they wanted to ask. Spinning his hat around his fingers, and looking a little ashamed, Billings said, "Thanks, Kip, for giving it to us straight – I don't suppose ..."

"What?"

"Maybe you'll get a little restless."

"How about you yourselves?"

"Oh, sure," Smiley said.

"How am I different from you?" he asked.

"That's right," Smiley said, and Kip chuckled as if they were a set of comic characters. It made them want to go. Shaking hands with him and patting him on the back, they left.

When they had gone Denis came downstairs and sat down beside his mother. Sober faced, steady eyes, they both watched him, as if he were a stranger they could never understand, who was likely to destroy them. His mother's body was rolling back and forth a little. She sighed, as if she knew all his past life and everything that was to happen to him. It was like the time when he was a boy and had stolen a bicycle and they came home together from the court. On that night years ago she had only sat very still, as she was sitting now.

"Don't stare at me like that. Why don't you say what you're thinking?" he said. His mother smiled a little.

"I know you better than anyone does, Kip," she said.

"Sure you do."

"I'm glad you're here with us, son."

"But you believe in me, don't you?" he asked simply.

"I believe in you, son."

"I do too, Kip," Denis mumbled shyly. But they didn't stop watching him. Sighing, he got his hat.

"Where are you going, Kip?" Denis said.

"Just out, just to be on the streets alone."

"Go out the back way or they'll see you," Denis said.

He went out the back door and swung himself over the fence into a lane. His feet scraped on the frozen cinders in the dark. The beautiful hum of the city began to make his head throb and he went out to the street. "If only they'll give me a chance to get along," he thought. "If only the papers don't make everybody scared of me. Please, dear Jesus, give me a chance, and all I ask is that people get a chance to know how I feel and that they don't keep away from me." At the corner near the bridge, he looked at the row of lights shining on the piles of snow along the river and glistening on the frosty gray faces of the great warehouses that had been there when he was a child. He looked at the path through the snow to the little corner tavern, and at the bare cold factory chimneys further down the river, thrust up in the heavy hanging sky. "O God, it's beautiful, dear Jesus, it's lovely! Look at those apartments on the other side of the river," he said. And he stood at the bridge, longing to cry out his gratitude to the men and women and children sleeping or dreaming or quarreling or loving each other in the lighted rooms in the houses on the other side of the river.

Three

WHEN HE woke up in the morning and heard the dripping of icicles and ice sliding off the roof he had a lust to be out in the street looking at the faces of passing people. Dressing, he hurried downstairs. His mother was moving slowly around the table getting his breakfast. She looked very tired, as if she had hardly slept.

"You know where I'm going, mom?" he said, knowing what she was thinking.

"Would it – would it be after the job?" she said, as if the job he had mentioned last night had stirred up some long-buried eagerness and hope that had kept her awake all night.

"Exactly," he said. "I'm going right over to the Coronet as soon as I have a bite to eat. It doesn't matter what kind of an old job it is as long as it lets me drift along like you and my brother and Tim, see?" He wanted to explain to her his desire for a simple life. As he talked her eyes brightened; for the first time in his life he made her feel a wish in him she understood. It brought her sudden passionate faith in him, and she began to cry softly.

"What's the matter?" he asked, surprised. "It's just like I'm telling you."

"It's nothing, nothing. I'm just glad that's all," she said.

It was almost magical the way they seemed to be close

together in a fine hope after years of separation. The wrinkled skin around her throat began to slip up and down. "Mom, mom, come on! Why don't you make me a cup of coffee and some toast like you used to do? You have a cup with me," he said. She used to wait up nights for him when he was a kid, and have a cup of coffee with him when he came in and insist that he tell her everything that had happened during the day.

While he ate his breakfast they talked with this same old eagerness. It made him feel suddenly that he had found his home again.

When he went out he looked back at the house and waved at the window. It was thawing out. A car, starting at the curb, was spraying snow all over the sidewalk as he came down the street. A little farther down he saw two girls coming along and he leaned against a lamp-post. He took out a match and chewed it and watched and listened while they passed. "Yeah, my father had to go out and rent a tuxedo," one was saying. Grinning, he threw the match in the snow and looked after them, wanting to follow them into their lives. At the corner there was a cake shop. The rich and lovely smell of baking bread made him stop and sniff. In the flat over the store a man was singing lustily. Looking up, he touched his hat. "O.K. Go to it, mister," he said.

He was passing the cigar store and he bought a paper at the newsstand. When he saw his picture on the front page he began to feel jittery. "It's what I was scared of," he thought, "Only it's bigger." His hands trembled as he leaned against the cigar store and tried to read the story. Smiley had told what he looked like, what he wore, the way he talked, the hope he felt. And alongside the story was a big smiling picture of the Senator. "Who'd want to give me a job with all this stuff in the papers?" he muttered miserably. "What's the use of going on to the hotel?"

Shaken, he threw the paper on the road and went into the store to get some cigarettes. When he was lighting one on the counter flame the little dark-haired clerk said shyly, "Excuse me, aren't you Kip Caley?"

"Yeah, I'm Caley," he said, looking away, dreading the sound of his own name.

"This is swell," the clerk said. He offered his hand over the counter. "I'm awfully glad to run into you."

"Eh?" he said, wondering, yet taking the clerk's hand.

"Good luck, Kip."

"You're glad to see me?" he said, unbelieving.

"You bet your life."

"Why?"

"I guess everybody's been waiting for you to come back – I remember when you went away. It's great to know you want to string along with everybody," the clerk said, with a lovely candid smile. Then grabbing a tin of cigarettes he said shyly, "Look, here's some cigarettes, you know – just for luck."

"Thanks – thanks," Kip said, taking the good-will offering awkwardly.

"I knew you by your pictures," the clerk said.

"In the papers – sure," he said. "Glad you saw it in the papers." Holding up the tin, he said, "Look at that. I'm going to keep that tin as long as I live. A lot of things come a guy's way in the world, but never anything nicer than that." He shook hands again very warmly and went out, feeling better than he did even before he saw the paper. He went on his way to the hotel.

Four

THE CORONET hotel near the university was a four-story, brick hotel used mainly by the second-class sporting trade. Across the street was a public dance hall. The hotel-keeper, Harvey Jenkins, wrestling and boxing promoter, had a string of wrestlers of his own. Squat, tin-eared, short-necked, heavy-shouldered men with bald heads were always going in and out of the Coronet. In the lounge there was always a group of young fellows gathered around some local lightweight who was promising to beat the ears off an imported punch-drunk third rater. During the racing season the hotel was crowded with men from far-away tracks with fine names like Blue Bonnets, Hialeah, and Tia Juana, who had been coming to the Coronet for years. Every day a special bus carried them out to the track and brought them to the hotel at night, or they could make their bets right in the hotel, for there was a wire direct to the track. With a dance hall just across the street, all the little tarts in town used to hang around there in the racing season.

When Kip came along the street, workmen on the scaffolds were cleaning the stone and brick front and painting the red brick till it shone like a great ruby in the brilliant light from the big new electric sign.

He went into the rotunda nervously and walked up to the desk. The pudgy boy with a puffy face and a cauliflower ear and thick hair parted in the center was smoking a cigar and sorting mail. He wheeled when he saw Kip. Staring at his big shoulders, he called, "Are you Kirelenko?"

"Me?" Kip asked.

"The big Russian burper the boss is waiting for?"

"Burper?"

"Rassler. Say, pal, where you been?"

"Out of town," Kip said.

"You a heavy? They won't look at heavies in this town. Too slow. That's my feeling too," he said, confidentially.

"My names's Caley, Kip Caley. I want to see Mr. Jenkins. He expects me," Kip said.

"Well, for Christ's sake, Kip Caley! Say, why didn't you say so? Say, why didn't I take a look at you? Why, my little brother and my old man have been talking about you all day." Leaning close, he said eagerly, "Maybe you remember me, eh? Billie the Butcher Boy, remember? What do you say?" His battered face brightened, hoping he would be remembered. "I went the limit with Kid Chocolate, remember?"

"I saw you take it from Chocolate," Kip said. Billie's arms were swinging automatically, his head was swaying, a glazed expression was in his eyes; he was sure he was still in there pawing away at Kid Chocolate. After these years it seemed terrible to see the kid behind the desk, blank-faced and starry-eyed, making those motions with his hands. "Heh, Billie," he called, "snap out of it. Where's the boss?"

"Here, put it there," Billie said, shaking hands. "They gave me a big play once too. Glad to see you getting a hand. Come on to the boss's office."

In the front office, where the windows overlooked the street, Jenkins was sleeping behind the desk. A glass of beer was on the table; the newspaper drooped from his hand. His chin had fallen on his chest and he snored and gasped uncomfortably for breath. He must have weighed nearly three hundred pounds. The skin on his face was drawn tight as a drum. His fatness was soft, alcoholic and unhealthy.

"He can't help it," Billie said. "You got to wake him. He goes off like that every half hour. It's got him scared. He keeps getting fatter and he can't help it. I call him the blimp, hoping he'll float away some day." Grinning, he shook Jenkins. It was funny the way the little blue eyes fluttered open. "Kip Caley's here, mister. He says you want to see him," Billie shouted.

"What's that? Yeah, yeah, you don't need to shake me. I heard every word you said," Jenkins said, rolling forward on his swivel chair.

"He's got the insomnia," Billie said apologetically.

"It gets my heart," Jenkins said. "I wasn't sleeping. I can't sleep. I mean I can't go on sleeping, not more than half an hour at a time."

"I knew a guy like that," Kip said.

"He's got to take off weight," Billie said.

"I'll be all right. I got three doctors working on me. I'll be all right when I take off eighty pounds," Jenkins said. Squeezing himself out of his chair, he sighed and grinned. "I been waiting for you. I phoned the Senator – great guy, the Senator. I thought you weren't going to show up," he said. Chasing Billie, he went on staring at Kip with his blinking, watery, tired blue eyes. Gradually, Jenkins' big, soft face grew very earnest. "It's like this," he said reassuringly, "I know all about you and I admire you. I like to think these things are happening all the time. That's what I said to the Senator. I said, 'This guy's no little run-of-the-mill punk. I got no business offering him a bus boy's job. He's a personality,' I said. And that's what you are, Kip, a personality."

"I don't get it."

"Like I said ..." He gasped for breath; the way he breathed painfully made him sound dreadfully eager. "I got the idea a week ago but I just played around with it, see? And it was only this morning when I was having my breakfast and reading the papers that I saw what a big thing it would be for both of us. The Senator asks me if I can find a job for you ... Anybody can put the touch on me.... You knew there was a job waiting for you didn't you?"

"That's what the Senator said."

"You're looking at the guy that was making it."

"I appreciate it," Kip said.

"No guy ever asked me for a lift and got turned down. But this morning I get this angle. I got thinking how much people liked meeting you down there. It's a talent you've got – ability to meet the public. A great talent, see?"

"You're kidding me," Kip said, and he grinned.

"That's quite a grin you've got," Jenkins said thoughtfully.

"I been smiling like that a long time," Kip kidded him.

"Is there something funny about me?"

"I think you're swell," Kip said.

"That grin of yours is worth money."

"How do you figure that?"

"That's just it. You're going to have a lot of people trying to figure it."

And then as if unfolding a very beautiful secret, Jenkins said softly, "This has always been a cosy little place, you understand. If I stuck to it I'd be doing well enough, though those rasslers have bellies like whales to fill. I also got a string of boxers, but they hardly more than pay for their feed with the fight game gone to hell around here, see? I promote a few boxing shows from time to time and I need someone to be around there all the time and meet people and see everything's going the right way, someone that – well, you know – someone that can give the place a little tone and authority. I've had something in my mind like this a long time, and I say to myself, 'He's that baby' – meaning you. Why? Because you like people – they'll like you."

"But what do I do?"

"A job like sort of looking after my new restaurant and floor show."

"But I don't know anything about restaurants."

"Am I asking you to do the cooking? You just greet the public, see? The main thing is you like people y' understand?" Jenkins' eyes began to close slowly, then they shot open. The desperate struggle going on in him between his desire to sleep and his eagerness to make a good bargain was frightening.

"I don't think I'd like it," Kip said.

"Fifty a week."

"But it's up the wrong alley. I'd be doing things every day that'd keep alive stuff I want to forget."

"Make it seventy-five."

"Look, Mr. Jenkins, I wouldn't want to take a job like this without talking to the Senator. It's not what he had in mind, and me neither. It's got me worried."

"Why, certainly you should talk to the Senator. Talk to him now. Use the phone– Go and see him."

"I mean he wanted me to work here, see, and it may not be the kind of job he had in mind. Maybe I'd better see him," he said. And he shook hands with Jenkins and promised to come back in a couple of hours.

Five

O N T H E W A Y down to the Senator's office in the Amal-
gamated Trust Building he was pretty worried. "How am
I going to sneak back into a normal life if I've got to be with a
flock of people all the time?" he kept asking himself. When he
went into the office and said to the little dark girl behind the
desk, "Caley's the name. Tell the Senator I'm here," she rose in
a slow pop-eyed motion. She led him into an immense office
with wide windows overlooking the lake.

Behind his big glass-top desk the Senator was waiting, and
he didn't look at all like the grave worried man who had
waited in the snow at dawn. All the papers were spread out on
his desk and he looked immensely pleased with himself. Over
near the window was another middle-aged, slightly bald-
headed man with a rosy contented face and a Roman collar
with a touch of crimson underneath it.

"Don't stand there, Kip," the Senator called. "Come in,
come in, we want to see you. Meet Bishop Murray." His weakness for doing things with a showy flair had been touched; he
wanted to share Kip opulently with the whole world. To the
Bishop he said, "Here he is, Your Grace – the lad himself."

The Catholic Bishop was there trying to negotiate some
mortgages on church property. It seemed to Kip that the
Bishop was trying to break into his thoughts with his shrewd

gray eyes and dig into his heart. He put his hand out hesitantly, almost begging the Bishop not to reject him.

"Well, well, Mr. Caley, hm, hm," the Bishop said, staring at Kip with bright curiosity. Of course, as a Christian he had to believe it possible in a man to change the pattern of his life, but he knew it hardly ever happened and he held aloof, curious, then he looked a bit ashamed. "I'm glad to see you, Caley," he said. Kip clasped his hand warmly.

"Now what about Jenkins, Kip?" the Senator said. "He just phoned me. He seemed a little disappointed. What did you do?"

"It was the job, a restaurant job, see? I wanted to get some place where nobody'd notice me. God knows how the thing would work out."

"Kip – Kip, don't talk like that," the Senator said. He seemed to be shocked. "Why are you always doubting things? Your Grace, he's always doubting things – he shouldn't do it, should he? I never doubt things – it's bound to affect the way things work out."

"I mean look at all those stories in the paper," Kip said. "What chance does it give me?" But the Senator's elation made him feel apologetic. There was no use trying to talk about the kind of a job it was, with the Bishop and Senator beaming at him happily.

"After all, they did a little feasting and celebrating for the prodigal son, didn't they?" the Bishop said indulgently.

"It's always a great story," the Senator said.

"That's funny," Kip said. He suddenly remembered the cigar store clerk's eager face and his beautiful good-will offering. "I guess people wanted to shake hands with the guy." And he smiled and pulled out the green cigarette tin. "See that," he said, "a guy in a store gives it to me this morning – just a gift, see?"

"How simple and beautiful," the Bishop said, and he seemed to be truly moved.

"Sure, it's just like I say – I can feel these things," the Senator said. "And here's another thing – I want you to come to the skating carnival with me – I phoned my tailor and told him you'd be around and get measured for some dress clothes. Fine clothes help a man, am I right, Your Grace?"

"Well, the body is the temple of the Holy Ghost. It ought to be adorned a little, I suppose," His Grace said.

"And now you're both coming to lunch with me," the Senator said.

"Why, sure," Kip said.

But the Bishop said uneasily, fearful of causing a scandal, "I think I should be going along. I don't think I have time."

"Ah, now Your Grace! At my club! And I'll close that mortgage deal right after lunch," the Senator promised.

"Very well," the Bishop sighed.

While the Senator got his coat and hat, and the Bishop puffed and sighed, buckling his galoshes, Kip was thinking they might have a better chance to talk about the Coronet job at lunch. But from the time they got out on the street they talked about nothing that could touch him. It made him feel like an invalid. He laughed, and startled the Bishop crossing the road when he slipped his arm under his and guided him past a street car. Going into the club he trailed them shyly. But when they were having a glass of sherry in the lounge and not one of the prosperous-looking business men stared at him he began to feel free. At lunch he hardly ate. He was happy; he was listening to the Senator twit the Bishop about his mortgages while the Bishop shook with contented laughter. "This isn't much like the hotel," he said suddenly and waited expectantly, but the Senator only laughed. Voices from other tables came to him talking about Hitler, Mussolini, the threat of Communism, the threat of Fascism, the threat of John L. Lewis. "This is wonderful," he thought. "No one pays any attention to me. Look at the big things they talk about here!" And their soft voices, their easy manners, their smooth faces and their assurance kept reminding him that this was the world he really wanted, and not the old hotel with the punch-drunk desk clerk.

He stayed there with them as long as he could, and when he was going, he tried again to tell them he was concerned about the job. "I've got to get back to Jenkins. He's waiting to see what you think," he said to the Senator.

"Tell him I want him to fix you up," the Senator said, "and remember – the carnival."

Six

WHEN HE got back to the hotel he stood in the snow looking at the entrance. A short, half-drunken little man with an overcoat far too big for him came out and lurched along, and a kid threw a snowball at him. Kip was waiting to get rid of his uneasy feeling about the place. With his hands in his pockets he walked up and down till his feet got cold, and then he went in. Jenkins was waiting for him and said, "Well, how do you feel about it now?"

"Not so good."

"What did the Senator say?"

"A Bishop was with him, and we didn't have much chance to go into it. He wasn't against it," Kip said. But he looked worried, himself.

Slipping his arm under Kip's, Jenkins said, "You don't have to make your mind up this minute. Come on and I'll show you the swell room I was going to give you."

On the way through the rotunda to the wide, unpolished oak stair Kip stopped to look at pictures of prize fighters and race horses on the walls. He liked everything the pictures suggested.

"Yeah, we get a great sporting crowd around here and you'd like them," Jenkins said, as if he knew Kip had always loved the hotels in the racing seasons when the lobbies were crowded with jockeys and trainers from far-away tracks.

The room on the second floor, a handsome room with gray broadloom carpet, modern furniture and two huge mirrors, wasn't the kind of a room Kip had expected to find in the hotel. He looked surprised. "This is all new, that's right," Jenkins said. "Downstairs gives a wrong impression of how the place is going to look. How do you like it?"

"It's a nice room," Kip admitted.

"Well, it's yours if you want it. Why don't you stay here a little while and get the feel of it, and then come down to the tavern where the floor show's working out and have a talk with me?" He shook hands warmly with Kip. And as if he had been suddenly pushed into a cage, Kip watched the door closing.

The room seemed to be a bright patch in the crazy quilt the place was. At the window he looked out at the dance hall sign and the bowling alley. In front of the grocery store a messenger boy was loading a basket of parcels on his bicycle. He said to himself, "Why, this place is a zoo. Maybe I should have gone to the zoo and watched the bears shuffling around behind the bars. At least the keeper wouldn't have offered me a cage." And he was disgusted. It seemed incredible that all the way on that journey through the last few years he should have been heading for this old sporting hotel where Jenkins was waiting for him.

Then someone tapped on the door and called, "Are you in here, Caley?" A squat, bald-headed man, who looked like a powerful ape, was coming over to him with his hand out. "I'm Steinbeck," he said, in a soft, sweet voice, his face full of simple friendliness. Kip liked him as soon as he heard him speak. "The boss asked me to come up and bring you down. He told me to have a talk with you. He says he wants to give you a good job and you don't know whether you should take it," and he started to laugh. Kip laughed too. "What's the matter with the place?" Steinbeck asked.

"It's not the place," Kip said apologetically, for he didn't want Steinbeck to think he had anything against a man like him. "But if you shove me into a greeter's job in a hotel like this, it sort of turns it into a menagerie." Hesitating, he said, "Wait a minute – you know who I am, don't you?"

"Sure, you're Caley."

"Yeah, and it looks as if a lot of old soldiers like Billie the Butcher Boy hang around here wearing their medals. Well, I'd be wearing mine, my jailbird's medal too, wouldn't I, shining it up for the customers?"

"So that's the angle," Steinbeck said, and he took a handful of raisins out of his pocket and began tossing them up and catching them in his mouth as he spoke. "What do you care who you are? What the hell. It's just a way of earning a living, isn't it? I run Jenkins' string of wrestlers for him. I'm Big Steinbeck, the strangler, see, and if you believe the cash customers, I kick the boys in the groin, gouge out their eyes and break their arms. Everybody hisses every time I step into a ring." He was grinning like a big happy boy. "But what's that got to do with me? I'm paid to make people feel that way about me – it doesn't touch me at all. I got a wife, I got three kids– It's just like swinging on a trapeze. If you earn your living at it do you need to be on it all the time?" Steinbeck's own good nature and simple dignity was obviously untouched by the burlesque character of his work. Kip was ashamed he had been thinking he would have been corrupted working in a hotel where Steinbeck lived. Whatever the job was, it should never trouble him. "It's all in the way you look at it," Steinbeck said, and he tapped his skull. "Good or bad, it's all in here. See, mister?"

Steinbeck's vast tolerance seemed to enfold him. He was a convict; Steinbeck, himself, was a phony villain – but that was all window dressing. They were essentially two friendly human beings walking along the corridor and going down the tavern together.

The tavern was a huge, new room with a separate entrance from the side street. Tables were piled high in a corner. Decorators were at work on the walls and ceiling, painting artificial oak beams that made the place look like an old English tavern. Near the platform at the end of the room Jenkins was sitting on a tilted chair listening to a tall Southern blues singer, who was shaking her head and saying bitterly to the man at the piano, "No, no, no, faster toward the end like I told you. Swing into it, da, da, da, da, da." As she pumped her arm up and down vigorously, Kip and Steinbeck sat down with Jenkins, tilting back in their chairs too.

"How do you feel about the job?" Jenkins asked.

"Well, I was thinking about it."

"What's the answer?"

"Well, supposing I try it for a couple of weeks," he said, thinking in this way he could please everybody and not be committed permanently to the job.

"That's fine – that's all I ask," Jenkins said enthusiastically. "If in a couple of weeks you don't feel – " but he almost choked on his words; someone had come up behind him and slapped him on the back. It was Smiley, from the *News*, standing behind them, bright-eyed.

"It's you I want to see, not the old entrepreneur here," he said to Kip. "They told me at your mother's place I'd find you here."

Kip didn't want to see Smiley because the story he had written might easily have spoiled everything for him. "Smiley – you turned out to be a cheap little squirt," he said.

"Heh, Kip, cut it out," Jenkins whispered. "The guy's a newspaperman, a friend of the house."

"Maybe he is," Kip said, but he said to Smiley, "I think what you did was rotten. The way a guy feels is sometimes terribly important to him, and no one should spoil it, and yet you stick it all over the front page."

"You got it wrong," Smiley said, and he seemed anxious to have Kip respect him. "Why, we got hundreds of letters about that story. You ought to see them – letters from mothers whose kids had turned out bad and are in jail and a whole army of people. Spoil it! My God, you don't get the significance of the thing!"

Kip looked at Jenkins to see if he believed Smiley, and he said, "That's pretty hard to figure. Still, if you got the letters ..."

"I got something bigger than that."

"Go ahead."

"We want your life story. I'll write it with you and we'll pay you twenty dollars a day for it and it'll run about a week."

"That's old stuff. People are sick of that," he said, pleading that they agree with him.

"Tell him you'll think it over, Kip," Jenkins urged him.

"There's no use," he said flatly.

"You can't keep it out of the paper," Smiley said. "Why don't you cooperate and have it in the way you want it?"

Kip said, "To hell with it."

"You've got a big complaint, haven't you?" Smiley said indignantly. "It wasn't the same with Steve Connick, was it?"

"Connick? What's the matter with Connick?" he said quickly. Connick was a scholarly forger whom he had worked with in the prison library and he had been very fond of him.

"Connick shot himself yesterday," Smiley said. "Didn't you hear? He ran out on the street and shot himself in the chest and his blood was all over the snow. He couldn't get on city relief on account of being on parole and he couldn't get a job, being an ex-convict. So his wife and kids are half starved and he's in the way. What price honesty, gentlemen?"

"Is he dead?" Kip asked him.

"No, he muffed it," Smiley grinned. "But when I was

reading all those letters about what you meant to the natives, I said to the boys that if they had a guy like you on the parole board Connick would never have shot himself."

"Me?" Kip asked innocently.

"Sure – you."

"You're kidding me," he said, laughing. But his eyes brightened. Smiley had touched a dream he had often had in prison, a dream of being free and being able to help discouraged jailbirds like Connick.

"Do you know anybody who could handle that kind of work better?" Smiley asked. "Isn't it along the line of work you were doing in the prison?"

Kip nodded, ready to change his feeling quickly if they were making a joke. Yet Smiley's voice sounded earnest; Jenkins certainly looked interested. In the prison Kip had been a liaison officer between the officials and prisoners, trusted by everybody. Now he seemed to hear the voices of some of his old comrades, who came to him about little and big things – "I've been saving that bit of soap for months and it means a lot to me." "If he doesn't give that comb back to me I'll cripple him. You'd better tell him, Kip." Even the warden asked him to talk to the men when they were discontented. He heard the cries of rioting convicts, the clang of metal on bars, the guards' threatening yells. He saw himself running to the warden, begging him to let him, a mediator, take a message to the men, who would trust him.

"How much were you going to pay for that story of mine?" he asked, smiling.

"Twenty dollars a day while it lasted. It'll be good for a week anyway."

"Listen – take the pay for the first three pieces around to Mrs. Connick this afternoon and pay her the rest at the end of the week and it's a deal."

"That's easy," Smiley said. "It's a deal. We'll get to work."

They all tilted back in their chairs, watching the adagio

dancers. Kip, banging his right fist slowly into the palm of his left hand, was thinking that if he had had a chance to have a talk with Connick, Connick would never have shot himself. He was not sentimental about convicts. He knew many prisoners were freed who were habitual criminals. But those who were like Connick ... "Me on the parole board!" he thought, looking around furtively. "He was kidding me, but someone could work with that board, someone jailbirds trusted and everybody else trusted." It would only be carrying on the work he had done among the men in the prison. He suddenly longed to believe it was possible. Then he mocked himself, he tried to blot the wish out of his heart. It kept coming back brighter. It enlarged everything. He found himself thinking that Jenkins' hotel was an interesting place to work, maybe the place where he should be. It spanned both sides of the tracks, the Senator's side and Connick's. He would be there, the middleman.

Seven

H<small>E HAD NOTHING</small> to do around the hotel for a few days while they were getting the place ready for the big New Year opening of the restaurant except sit around talking with Jenkins and Steinbeck. The glimpse he had got in the Senator's club of a great world where men talked about significant events still stirred him. He wanted to be in it again. He began to look forward to going to the skating carnival. Worrying about getting his dress clothes, he phoned the tailor three times.

When he put his dress clothes on and looked at himself he felt proud. He wanted to show himself to people close to him who could share his delight. And on the way to the carnival he went over to his mother's house, a big happy grin on his face. When he went in, he bumped into Denis in the hall, carrying his doctor's bag.

"Is it the old lady?" Kip asked him.

"I just gave her something to put her to sleep. I wouldn't disturb her now," Denis said.

"Is her heart bad – worse than it was?"

"You know she's bad. I only give her a few months to live – the muscles of her heart are worn out." Looking sourly at Kip's clothes, he pushed past him.

"Wait a minute. What's so funny about me?"

45

"The fancy get-up."

"What's the matter with it?"

"Sh, sh, she'll hear us," Denis said. But Kip resented Denis' sourness and grabbed his arm.

"Come on, what have you got to say? Let's hear it," Kip said.

"It's not funny to me," Denis said.

"You've been ducking me for days."

"I get it all in the papers, don't I?" Denis said, watching Kip's big wild face. "Why didn't you go away and forget yourself? Why stick around here and let that big tycoon, Senator Maclean and his friends have a field day with you? Maybe he's generous, but he's irresponsible. They're all irresponsible...."

"And where would I be now if it wasn't for him?" Kip said.

"Well ..."

"Go on, answer me, Dr. Ritchie, Dr. Ritchie." He mocked him for changing his name. Denis backed away, as if Kip was going to hit him. They were close together in the hall, Kip towering over him, feeling a vast loyalty to men with good will like the Senator and his friends.

"I guess I shouldn't say anything, Kip," Denis said. "It's no thanks to me you're here. You never felt I was very close to you. I know you're as good as anybody else – and you're generous and impulsive– But all that won't get a man to first base. It's the way things shape up around him."

Kip realized how close his brother must have always felt to him and his voice broke as he said, "I guess we both try and do it the way we see it."

"Sure," Denis said.

"Come around and see me...."

"Not at those prices," Denis said. "So long." And he went out.

Kip stood in the hall, wanting to go in and wake his mother, yet knowing he shouldn't, and feeling the night was spoiled. He put on his hat and buttoned up the coat he had opened wide to show his dress shirt and started to go out. But Tim, coming from the kitchen, called shyly, "Uncle Kip, see this ball?"

"You a ball player?" Kip asked idly.

"Sure, I pitch."

Suddenly anxious for simple friendship, he rubbed Tim's head and said in a soft voice, "Do you kids like to hang around the hotel where the ball players stay? Do you like being there in the evenings after the ball game when the team comes home from the stadium and it's getting dark?"

"Sure we do," Tim said, fingering the stitches on the baseball, gripping it with his fingers. "See this ball – well – the kid that owns this ball – Joe Myers, see, well – he wondered if you'd autograph it for him. I wouldn't ask you, only I sort of promised the guy I could get you to do it." He looked pretty worried.

Kip took the ball in his hand, looked at it, and said to Tim, "Why does he want me to sign this?"

"It would be swell for him to have, wouldn't it?"

"Why me? I'm not a ball player."

"Well, gee, you're a bigger guy than any ball player."

"No, no, I'm not," he whispered. "You've got it wrong, Tim. I'm not a big guy." He wanted to explain it but he kept thinking of Denis and his coldness, and suddenly Tim's splendidly simple admiration became very precious to him. He was afraid to say anything for fear of mixing him up. He was afraid to touch it at all. "We'll be pals, eh?" he said, rubbing Tim's head again, and the curse Denis had put on the evening seemed to be taken off.

"Can I walk along with you a piece, Uncle Kip?"

"Geez, no. I got to grab a taxi, I'm late now," he said.

Eight

ONLY A FEW people, late like himself, were hurrying into the gardens. He followed the usher along the aisle in front of the row of boxes. In the darkness he couldn't see the occupants. The ice glistened in the spotlight. There was no sound but the cutting of skates on ice. The world's champion figure skater from Vienna was pivoting with his arms folded, one knee raised, the lights glistening on his oiled black hair and on his white silk blouse. In a roar of applause the lights came on and Kip was standing alone in the aisle, startled, looking up at rows of white shirt fronts, velvet evening gowns, bald heads and eager-faced girls. They all seemed to be staring at him. Then he saw the Senator standing up in his box, waving, and he rushed to him like a kid to a shelter out of the rain.

With the Senator was his daughter, Ellen, with bobbed blonde hair, a short round face, a short nose, and rather small, bright, blue eyes that wrinkled attractively at the corners. He was very glad that the lights went out before they had a chance to speak to him.

"This is Kip, Ellen; my daughter, Kip," the Senator was saying.

In his low rumbling voice Kip said, "Glad to meet you, Miss Maclean." And he squeezed into his seat beside her.

Out on the ice they were doing a ballet. The ice was

48

suddenly flooded with violet, the costumes of the ballet absorbing all light but the violet ray. The ballet formed bright violet patterns on the silver ice sheet in the darkness. He had never seen anything like it, yet it seemed a natural part of the new world he was in and it delighted him. But he kept feeling the Senator's daughter beside him, feeling how smooth and expansive she was, remembering the glimpse of her sullen little face. She was as strange to him as the violet pattern in the darkness. When the lights came on she was smiling at him, her eyes bright with curiosity.

"I'm glad you came," she whispered.

"So am I," he said.

"I hear you'll be at the Coronet, New Year's Eve."

"That's right."

"We'll certainly be there rooting for you."

Leaning over them, the Senator said, "I don't think you made a mistake taking that job, Kip. If you give it a thought or two you'll get another slant on it. It's audacious, that's the main thing. That's what I like, audacity, audacity. Challenge the town's imagination."

"I didn't know anything about a restaurant or night club, Senator," Kip said.

"Oh, nonsense! Let Jenkins worry about that!"

Kip knew the Senator was feeling different than he did that morning on the road from the prison when maybe he had wondered why he let his impulsiveness dominate his life. His curiosity seemed to have been deeply stirred. It seemed to fascinate him to watch the way the thing he had started was working out. It had become a strangely exciting intellectual adventure.

"Here's a program, Kip," he was saying. "Everybody comfortable? Tell him all about it, Ellen. We're all mighty glad to have you with us, Kip."

"Daddy's making a speech," said Ellen lazily. Leaning close to him she laughed and he didn't know whether she was mocking him or her father. The way she laughed made her seem very spoiled, important and aloof, and somehow more beautiful. "Would you mind if I asked you a question, Mr. Caley?" she whispered.

"Go ahead, Miss Maclean, anything you want."

"Oh, I'm sure no one has asked you this before."

"I'll answer it if I can."

"Promise?"

"It's a go."

"Well, listen," she whispered. "Do you ever feel like robbing a bank?"

"No, Miss Maclean, I don't."

"I guess nobody ever asked you that before," she said, chuckling.

"A man feeling like I do doesn't go around with those crazy thoughts," he said earnestly. But the lights went out. On the ice the woman champion from London, in a gold dress, was drifting by with her leg thrust back and her body forward in one smooth horizontal line, the spotlight following her lovely long leg and gleaming on her golden skirt. The gentlemen in the boxes trained their opera glasses on her lovely leg as she glided off, and applauded enthusiastically. After her came all the members of the skating club trailing on the ice for a burlesque hunting number with a dog for a fox and little brown-coated boys with tails for dogs and many canvas horses with two skaters in each one.

Kip was waiting to tell Ellen how silly her question was, but when the canvas horses and the brown-coated boys began to jump awkwardly over the ice he felt his earnestness was unreal in this fairy ice-palace. Her interest in him seemed to belong in this world of colored prancing figures sliding around stiffly on skates.

The Senator was droning away to a friend in the next box. "With that geological formation there's simply got to be ore there. Thompson's never been wrong ... Give them a chance

… Why, they've only been drilling a month … Did you see the samples in my office?"

"There's something else I was wondering," Ellen whispered.

"Yeah."

"Was it true that you used to really like robbing banks?"

"I guess I liked it at the time."

"What was the kick you got out of it?"

"The excitement, I guess," he said restlessly.

"That's what everybody wants, isn't it?"

"I figure I wanted it in a big way."

"But listen," she whispered eagerly, "won't you be missing all that excitement? I would."

"No – I got something better now."

"What?"

"Just a pretty good feeling," he said, feeling stupid.

"What gives it to you?"

"Just another way of looking at things, see?"

"No – I don't see."

"A guy's got to have something that makes him tick, something he believes in."

"That's not so bright," she whispered.

"Well –" he began helplessly.

"I'm interested, please go on – I'm simply intrigued," she said. But that big vital flow of words would not come. He felt himself being knotted up. She seemed to be picking away at him, winding a web around him, this little smooth girl, this tiny little girl like a doll in the dark beside him.

And then the lights came on. It was intermission and the ladies and gentlemen were promenading in the aisle, bowing to the Senator and Ellen. Streaming past, they stared at Kip. Everything seemed to brighten for him. A man in an opera cloak lined with white silk, the financial editor, J.J. Williams, and his young wife, who was ruining him with her expensive social climbing, came up to Ellen, their faces glowing.

"Hello, hello, hello," Ellen said, enjoying herself. "I want you to meet Kip Caley."

When they shook hands with him, he became startled and backed away. Worried, he swung, around, looking for a passage to the exit. But a little crowd had gathered in the aisle. They smiled and whispered. The tightness in him was becoming unbearable and spoiling this world for him. All their faces seemed to belong to the glistening ice, the violet lights, the stiffly jumping horses. These faces were bright masks. The Senator's mask was pink and white. Ellen had on a sharp, pretty little frozen-faced mask. Kip felt he was incredible. They gaped up at him as if he were a great crag of basalt. Snatches of conversation in polite voices came to him, "What a big, handsome brute he is! What are the Macleans up to?" "He's splendid, but think of being up an alley with him if he hated you!" "There you are – right under your eyes – moral grandeur, my dear." "Look at the pallor of his face!" "That's the prison pallor." And the knot that Ellen had tied in him was now so tight his heart seemed to be bursting. He said jerkily, "Did I tell you I had a date? Did I tell you I had to go at half time?"

"Oh, you can't go," Ellen pouted. "You've got to come out afterwards and have something to eat with us."

"I can't, Miss Maclean," he said, stuttering, and feeling he would have to push her away from him. "I've got to go, I'm late for my date."

"Oh, please, just for me," she coaxed.

But the Senator slapped him on the back and said heartily, with everybody listening, "Go ahead, lad. We can see you again. I hope you had a nice time," and he smiled happily.

"Thanks, thanks –" he said, and he shook hands nervously and hurried out with his head down.

Nine

IT HAD GOT much colder out, the slush on the sidewalk was in hard ruts, and as he walked along with his head down against the full wind from the north he was terribly worried about the way he had shown his excitement in the crowd. Long ago he had figured out it was when he was excited that he got into trouble. He used to do things to break the tension that tied him up. Looking for a bright little place to read a newspaper, he went down the street. He got a paper on the corner. Three blocks south he came to a black and white lunch counter. He went in, ordered a sandwich from the girl and spread the paper out on the counter.

"My God, what's the use of running away from it?" he thought, for there was his story of prison life running on the front page. In another column some of the leading Protestant ministers told what they thought of his reformed life. He read the paper nervously. His wonder grew. One of the ministers, Dr. Carlton Ross, quoted from the sermon he was going to preach the coming Sunday on "Kip Caley – A Change of Heart." The young Rabbi Goldstein spoke eloquently about human fellowship and society's open door for the disinherited. Only one, the popular Dr. Howard Stevens, had no time to discuss the matter. "All my time is taken up with such world problems as international peace," he said grandly.

Kip began to feel very glad and grateful. He was ashamed of having fled from the carnival. Those people who gazed at him had probably been only thinking the same things these ministers were saying. He remembered Smiley saying people had written moving letters to the paper. It all seemed to touch his secret dream of working with the parole board, the dream he dared not believe in. Laughing at his eagerness, he looked out the window, watching the flakes of hard snow whirling down the street, whirling in a hard-driven horizontal slant across the window.

"There's your sandwich," the girl said.

"Eh?"

"Your sandwich."

"Oh, sure," he said, smiling at the clean, small, white-aproned girl with black hair in loose curls on her forehead. Her dark eyes were wide apart and intelligent, but it was her mouth that made her beautiful.

A cold wind hit him on the back of the neck, and two young fellows, red-cheeked from the cold and in white ties and tails like himself, came in puffing and blowing and laughing and filling the place with the smell of whiskey. The plump, dark boy, putting his elbows on the counter, sighed. "Come on, Tubby, we've got places to go yet," his friend said.

"A cup of black coffee," Tubby said to the girl.

"Me, too, sister," the fair lad said. "Coffee and ham on rye."

As she turned to the big nickel boiler, standing with one hand on her hip, the fair boy took off his top hat and whispered, "My God, she's beautiful. Look, Tubby, look at her neck." When she put the black coffee in front of them, Tubby stared at her and her faced reddened.

"Little one, this is a dump, a joint, a hamburg wagon, you shouldn't be here," he said.

But the girl only shrugged and Tubby grinned and said, "She's proud, see?"

The boys seemed to have come out of the Senator's friendly

world and Kip grinned at them. The fair boy gave the girl a dollar bill. When she gave him the change in a little pile of silver, he started to laugh, looking at it a long time, then he pushed it toward her.

But just as she went to touch it, he shot out his hand, covered the money and pointed. "Ah, ah, ah," he baited her. Ashamed, she turned away. "So you turned commercial on us, eh?" he said. And he and his friend laughed crazily.

"Beautiful but corrupt, I guess," Tubby said sadly.

"The taint of money."

"Finish your coffee, college boys," she whispered.

But Kip wanted to have her smile and make it a joke, and not look sullenly at the money under the boy's smooth hand as if she was thinking of all the times she had wanted to be with boys like them.

When they stopped laughing, plump-cheeked Tubby said, "Oh, don't mind him, lady; he's stingy, that's all."

"Me stingy!" his friend said indignantly. "I never in my life gave a damn for money, and you know it. You amaze me, my friend."

"Give it to her then."

"I say I have a great contempt for money. I want that on the record."

"I never did believe it, my friend."

Kip thought they were working themselves up to give the girl some money and he was glad and laughed at them.

"Look, lady," the fair boy began, "I'd have let you keep that change, but you were too quick on the draw. Not much, just a little. I'm a man with a generous heart. Look," he said. Taking four silver quarters from his pocket, he dropped one in his coffee, smiling brightly at his friend, and the three he had left he tossed up and down in his palms, jingling them. Doubtfully, his friend took a two-dollar bill from his pocket and held it in his hand, too.

As the girl pretended to be arranging a few dishes on one of the shelves, her eyes brightened with anxiety, and Kip longed to see the boys give her the money and see her surprised smile.

"Look, lady," the fair boy said. He tossed the silver up and down. In spite of herself she half turned, her head down, watching the coins in his palm, and everything that Kip had ever wanted seemed at that moment to be held in the boy's palm, all the things he had wanted when he used to lie awake in his cell dreaming of nights of freedom when freight trains rumbled through the hills. And he whispered to himself, "Go on, son. Give it to her."

"I have contempt for money," the fair boy said. With a little splash he dropped one of the coins in his cup of coffee. Stiff against the counter, hating them, her eyes showed her humiliation.

He could hear Denis saying earlier that evening, "Irresponsibility – thoughtless irresponsibility." He knew it had touched Steve Connick, but here it was right under his eyes as the girl turned to him with a stricken little smile, the only one who might help her.

"The stupid arrogance of some people's kids," she whispered. But he wanted to smooth it out between her and them and he leaned over the counter, wishing she would come close to him, wanting to say, "Take it easy, kid. Don't look at them like that. You've got it wrong a bit. Anybody from either side of the track is apt to be pretty thoughtless. They're mighty nice boys. They're just trying to show off."

Reaching for the sugar bowl, the happy fair boy poured some in his coffee and said, "Like this, see," and then he dropped in another coin and poured in more sugar, his face brightening childishly. As the coffee finally spilled over the rim, he said triumphantly, "There, Tubby, what do you think?"

"Why, that's sweet – that's an interesting point to make. Money is sweet," Tubby said with a half drunken comical seriousness. He opened his sandwich solemnly and laid his two-dollar bill between the slices of bread and started to munch them.

But the girl could stand it no longer, her eyes were wild; she tried to jeer at them and laugh, but she couldn't seem to get her breath. She suddenly shouted, "You cheap little show offs – you chuckle-headed smart alecks," pounding her fist on the counter. Her vehemence startled them all. Kip was terribly glad. He was completely disgusted with the boys.

But the boys only gaped at her, and he got up and went closer, towering over them. "Get out quick or I'll throw you out," he said. And he was so big, his face looked so hard, the two lads backed away scared. But Tubby remembered his two-dollar bill in the sandwich; keeping his frightened eyes on Kip, he fished the bill from the slices of bread. "Hurry!" Kip shouted. They jumped and ran to the door. As they opened it he grabbed the coffee mug in his hands and pitched it out the door at them. It broke on the road. From the kitchen the Greek came running, looking out at the boys' frightened faces. There was the sound of their mocking laughter; then they were gone.

"What goes on?" the Greek asked.

"A couple of kids tight," Kip said.

"They pay?" he said quickly to the girl.

"They paid," she said.

"O.K., let them go," he said. Looking up at the clock he said: "Twelve, eh? I guess you go now," and he went back to the kitchen.

The girl's eyes were closed as she leaned back against the shelf, her lips were tight together and she was trembling, trying to keep from crying.

"It's all right, kid," he said.

"I know. It's nothing. Many thanks."

"They had a sniff at a cork, that's all."

"Why did you jump in there like that?" she said, puzzled.

"I figured you wanted the money pretty bad, maybe I'm

wrong," he said. "It was that look you had on your face, see? I know what it is like. I've wanted things pretty bad myself."

"Thanks, Mr. —— "

"The name's Caley – Kip Caley," he said, uneasily.

"Well, thanks, Mr. Caley," she said.

And he gaped at her, hardly believing she didn't know him. She was getting her hat and coat off the peg, and if she went, that little touch of elation he felt being unknown would go too. "I figured you were new at the joint," he said quickly.

"How can you tell?"

"The way you handle the cups – like you were afraid of breaking them. You've got to learn to push them around."

"Thanks again," she said, "I'll remember." And she took a mirror from her purse and put lipstick on, and shoved her brown felt hat carelessly on the side of her head. Magically it seemed to belong there. She put on a loose brown coat, which was more like a spring coat and not nearly heavy enough for that winter night, but which must have been very expensive once.

"Could I walk along with you?" he asked timidly.

"I just live a few blocks away."

"I'd certainly like to, miss," he said; and his voice was so earnest, she started to laugh.

They went out together, and the broken coffee mug and two of the silver quarters were in the gutter and the falling snow was beginning to cover the fragments. From the north the wind whirled the snow so hard against them that they had to hold their hats on and duck their heads, and when they were crossing the road and he took her arm his heart began to beat like a boy's. It was long since he had walked with a girl. Yet he couldn't even see her face. Just the tip of her nose showed, with her chin tucked down in her collar. Her name was Julie Evans, she said.

She lived in an apartment overlooking the school yard on Temple Street. When they were in the hall, at the foot of the worn stair with the brass strips on the edge of the steps, she drew away from him a little shyly, saying good night. He went to kiss her, but she shook her head. The way she swung away from him made him feel he was losing her. He grabbed hold of her and kissed her. Pulling back, she stared at him, then smashed him on the face with her handbag and ran up the stairs.

"Wait, wait," he called desperately. Leaping up the stairs after her, he caught her on the first floor, when she was turning the key in the lock of her apartment.

"I just couldn't help it. Don't be sore at me. Say you aren't sore. I wouldn't hurt you. You looked so pretty, that's all. I didn't intend to do it. Just let me talk to you," he blurted out. She was closing the door on him and he grabbed her wrist.

"Let go, you big turkey," she said.

"I just wanted to tell you …"

"I can tell you more about you and your crowd than you can take, mister," she said. When she found she couldn't break the grip of his big hand she glared at him.

"Look, you're just a kid, I wouldn't hurt you," he pleaded.

"I just need to yell and they'll throw you out of here, you phony," she said. "What do you think this is? What were you doing back there? Maybe the other two boys were just stooges for you, the big front, eh – the lot of you taking a night off slumming." Her contempt for everything she thought he stood for came leaping out at him freshly. He hadn't met anyone like her since he was a kid. "Get out! Are you going to get out?" she said. She gave him a violent shove, but he didn't budge, and then she whispered, "Please …"

"What?"

"Please go," she said so softly he could hardly hear her. There were tears in her eyes. The hurt she had been enduring all night finally broke her. She looked like a helpless kid.

"Say, don't cry. What's the matter? I was going. You could call a cop. I just liked being here with you. I grabbed you like

that on the stair because I thought I might never see you again
– it scared me."

"What do you want?" she said sullenly.

"Just to talk."

"I don't feel like talking. I'm tired," she said. But she walked
over to the couch with the green shawl thrown over it and sat
down and took out her handkerchief and dabbed at her nose,
watching him suspiciously.

"I don't blame you for being sore," he said, coaxing her.
"You thought I was just another tramp in a high hat, eh? You
don't know how much I was with you in the restaurant, sort of
talking to you all the time. I was with you, wasn't I?"

"Yes."

"Well, then …"

"You sound like a pretty smooth guy to me."

"Was I smooth at the lunch counter?"

"No, you were sweet. I liked you then," she said.

Her savage candor flustered him, and he walked awkwardly over to the window and looked out at the snow whirling white in the separate glow of each street light. Then he
looked around the room at the folding table with the books on
it, the bright colored French prints on the wall with their dis-
torted figures. Finally he reached up and touched the top of
the high window and said awkwardly, "I guess you never saw
anybody as big as me, eh?"

"That's right," she said.

"You noticed it, eh?"

"It's hard to miss," she said, smiling a little.

While she sat there looking beaten, he was waiting for her
to be engrossed in his size, and he felt ashamed. He sat down
looking worried, his big hands hanging between his knees.
The snow was melting on his hat. He shook it and sent a little
spray of snow drops on the floor.

"What was the matter, kid?" he asked gently.

"I told you. I've been pretty nervous."

"But you seem to have such a big grudge against people."

"It just hasn't been going so well with me."

"Since when?"

His eagerness to be close to her she couldn't understand. She said hesitantly, "Since I've been sick. I was a model. I had been at it for about a year, but I had a breakdown. I got thin and out of touch, and the agencies have about a million girls in line anyway. Besides I didn't feel particularly anxious to go back."

Though she distrusted him, his gentleness seemed to make her feel that everything that had happened to her was important to him. She was smoothing her skirt with the flat of her hand, as if troubled by her own willingness to talk to him.

"Modeling wasn't steady and I was green at it, and I tried to work the sidelines, posing and getting pushed around by out-of-town buyers and getting soaked in gin – it was terrible waking up in the mornings...." She was crouched on the bed now, and one round silk-stockinged knee showed in the slope of her young body to her small round breast. The soles of her shoes were still wet from the snow. In one sole there was a little hole showing a bit of wet paper shielding her stocking. "I thought it was all adding up to something – I guess I cracked – I never wanted to see a cloak and suit man again. Everything seemed to be cheapened."

"You're just a swell believing kid," he said gently. "I thought you had a grudge."

"I have," she said. "I got to hate the way everybody admitted money was the only important thing." And then she smiled. "Maybe I'm taking a crack at you." She nodded at his dress clothes.

"These clothes?" he asked, astonished.

"Sure– Say, what are you anyway?"

"I'm just getting started – kind of a new line," he said awkwardly.

"A big bootlegger maybe?"

"Aw, come on. Give me a break."

"A big promoter?"

"I sort of work in a hotel," he said.

"I knew it was something like that," she said. "That's perfect." She linked her hands behind her head. She said candidly, "Just the same you've got a pretty soothing bedside manner. Are you getting much of a kick out of listening to me?"

"I bet you're not twenty," he said.

"And I'm sour, sure."

"We all get pushed around," he said.

"You look it," she said. "It's been a pretty soft touch for you, mister."

But he was scared to tell her who he was. The window rattled loudly as the wind drove against it. They both turned and looked at it.

"A guy feels a little sour," he said, "and wants to pull away from everybody. He starts hating people. He goes off on his own – like you feel now. But he's got to come back, or he might as well quit. You come back, wondering if anybody'll give you a break, and you find a few people glad to see you. Maybe we're all prodigal sons, everybody on earth, see, going away places and feeling homesick and wanting to come back."

"Go on, mister, you're doing swell," she said, amused.

"Your shoe's got a big hole in it," he said, embarrassed.

"I get it. You're a shoemaker looking for business."

"Yeah, that's right. I was a shoemaker," he said. "Let's see it."

She pulled the damp shoe off and there was a big round wet spot on her stocking. Looking earnestly at the shoe, he held it up against his eyes. He could see her head through the hole. They both began to laugh.

"Sure, I could fix it," he said.

"Why don't you go home?" she said.

"I like sitting here."

"Go on home."

"I'm not hurting you. Let me sit here," he pleaded with her.

In this room with her lying there smiling at him and the window rattling, he suddenly lost his identity. For the first time in years he knew the peacefulness that comes from being anonymous. He began to talk about anything that came into his head, his deep voice friendly and close to her. But at last she said, "I'm sleepy, I'm sorry, I'm sleepy. It's all right for you, but I've got to work in the morning."

"It's early," he said.

"Please go home," she said.

"I'll go, take it easy," he said. But her eyes were beginning to look red-rimmed. "Just a sleepy kid, eh," he teased her, getting up to go.

"What's the name of the hotel?" she said.

"The Coronet," he said uneasily.

"Happy New Year, Mr. Hotelman."

"Happy New Year," he said.

Ten

H E DIDN'T go back to see her because Jenkins had put placards with his picture all over town. On New Year's Eve he stood with Jenkins at the window in his office watching the crowd come in. The big doorman in the blue uniform was sheltering the fur-coated ladies with his huge umbrella from the wet heavy snow. Lifting their faces in the snow they looked up at the big flickering sign. Their faces all looked red and excited in that light.

"It's simply marvelous," Jenkins said. "The whole town's coming here."

"Maybe they'll laugh at me," Kip said.

"My God, no! You're a personality. You don't seem to get it."

"What do I have to do?"

"Just be friendly with them. I don't want to spring you on them till nearly midnight, y' understand? The New Year – see – a beautiful backdrop for you. You standing up there with the whole God-damned New Year ringing in on you, see. Stick around in here a while till I come and get you," he said and hurried out.

Alone with the laughing voices drifting up from the street and the music from the colored swing band coming from the restaurant, he knew if they laughed he couldn't stand it. The

sound of his feet padding on the carpet as he walked up and
down made him feel he was in a cage. Then the peacefulness
he had felt that night in Julie Evans' room began to seem mar-
velously beautiful. He remembered her worn shoe. "I should
send her a pair of shoes," he thought. Wanting to do something to take his mind off the hotel he thought, "I should to it
right now."

He got his coat and hat and sneaked down the stairs, out
the side door and along the other side of the street, looking for
a shoe store. The wet snow melted on his face. His low dress
shoes sank in the thick snow. The curtain of snow, draping all
the lighted store windows in white made them all look alike
and he went farther and farther away from the hotel, crossing
the road, looking all around. When he found a shoe store they
were turning out the lights. But he rattled the door and they let
him in. He bought a pair of brown shoes, size four A, with
spike heels, and a pair of gray fur-trimmed galoshes.

"Send them to that address and put a card in and say – from
the shoemaker, see?" he said to the surprised clerk. And then
grinning to himself, feeling very good about everything, he
began to hurry back to the hotel. He waved to passing taxis,
but it was New Year's Eve and they were all full of people
shouting and singing. He began to run, squashing through the
snow with his huge strides, his stiff collar getting limp, his
clothes sticking to him, till he saw the big red ruby glow of the
hotel in the veil of snow and heard the music.

Going slowly because the place was filled with shouts and
laughter, and the lobby crowded, he was half way up the stairs
before Jenkins shouted, "Kip, for God's sake. This is terrible.
Give me your coat."

"What happened?"

"Where were you?"

"Buying a pair of shoes."

"Mayor Wills is here. He came with Senator Maclean. It's
wonderful. And he's got to go. Hurry and we'll catch him."

They were running down the stairs together arm in arm. "Thank God. There he is just coming out," Jenkins said.

Mayor Wills, a little, pudgy, pompous man was coming to him with his hand out.

"This is a pleasure," the Mayor said.

"Many thanks, sir. I hope you have a happy New Year," Kip said.

People came crowding out the restaurant and gathered around them.

"I'm mighty proud of the way it worked out for you, Caley," the Mayor said. "What's happened to you is the thing our system stands for." The Mayor was an admirer of Senator Maclean, who had made him a lot of money on gold mining stock. "Come and see me some day, Kip," he said.

"Why, geez, I'd be delighted."

"Come any time. You've probably got a lot of good ideas about prison conditions." Patting Kip on the shoulder, pretending to be very serious, he said, "And don't forget to let me know the next time you're going to stick up a bank – I want to get in on it with you." The little group burst into laughter.

"Sure, sure," Kip said, surprised. Then he laughed too.

"He's a peach, and a great kidder," he said to Jenkins. "You think he meant that about me going to see him, don't you?"

"Sure he did, and you be sure and go and see him," Jenkins said.

But the crowd around them was getting larger and Jenkins said, "Damn it all, this spoils my plans. If you don't go in there now everybody'll get sore." He looked worried. "I got it – sneak in and sit with the Senator and lay low. Go on," he whispered.

Kip tried to slide in around the palm trees near the door, but everybody seemed to be rising up from the tables. He ducked furtively. Somebody screamed, "There he is behind the tree." Full of enormous surprise he stood still, his face set in a cracked, bewildered smile. The whole city seemed to be reaching out to grab him while he stood lost and helpless, trying to locate the Senator. "Jesus Christ," he gasped. "What do they want?" Then he saw the Senator a little farther away with Ellen and a middle-aged publisher, waving his hand like a delighted magician; the only one in the world who seemed close to him.

"Here we are, Kip, here, here," the Senator was calling. People reached their hands out and touched him as he sat down, trembling.

"Boy, oh, boy," he said. "What is this?"

"I've never seen anything like it," the Senator said.

The publisher had his hand out and Ellen, her sullen little face bright with animation, whispered, "Daddy said you'd sit with us and here you really are." But he only looked at them blankly. Everything was coming at him too fast.

"I saw the Mayor," he said. "He was swell. He wants me to go and see him. What do you know about that?"

"He wouldn't be smart if he didn't," the Senator said. "You're his whole social program walking around the streets."

"Gee, it's a wonderful big thing to have the head man in a city believing in you like that," he said.

From the tables all around they began to call in hoarse whispers, "Oh, Kip, come on and say hello."

Turning round slowly he let them see him. The grin on his face was a little cracked and crazy-looking. At the table behind him was a round rosy-faced Greek with big black moustaches, who was sitting with his wife, and who had kept calling, "Meester Caley – Meester Caley." The earthy warmth of the Greek's face suddenly made everything seem natural. "How ya doing?" Kip said, holding out his hand to the Greek.

"I'm Christopholous – Nick Christopholous – I've got a restaurant – and – I'm touched – I'm touched right here," he said, tapping his heart with his palm.

"I'm just as glad to meet you, Nick."

"Me ..."

"You bet."

The Greek beamed at him. "Wait – it just hits me," he cried. "Tomorrow I make a special sandwich. I call it the Kip Caley sandwich – a gesture for peace, freedom – international, see? How's that?" he asked grandly.

"You'll drive all your customers away," Kip said. But as he stood up and looked around he was laughing.

"Here, Kip, over here!" someone else was calling. "Here, over here." They were all putting on yellow and green and red paper hats. They were getting drunk and blowing whistles. Forgetting that Jenkins had told him to wait till midnight he got up and went among them.

As he passed, people said: "What do you make of him?"

"Did you see his eyes?"

"He's smooth, all right."

"Doesn't he make you feel he's very important?"

"Maybe he is."

As he passed the table of one of the prosperous shoe merchants, J. C. Henderson, a plump and confident man, with a high, sloping forehead, who was sitting with a vaudeville dancer, he begged him, "Have a drink with us, Mr. Caley."

"Maybe I will later."

"My name's Henderson, Henderson shoes. You've heard of the Henderson last, I presume?"

"I'll bet it's a good shoe."

"An educational shoe. Ever suffer from arthritis?"

"Never in my life."

"If you ever do, come and see us. But I was just wondering something sitting here watching you …"

"Go ahead, Mr. Henderson," Kip said. And he seemed to make the shoes and the little conversation very important.

"Well, what I've been wondering is – do you ever get the urge to go out and rob a bank?"

"His interest is merely scientific," the girl said with a sly wink.

"Like a kid wanting to set off a firecracker, eh?" Kip said. "No, mister, I've got a new bunch of firecrackers. They're going off all the time. Pop, pop, pop! Just like that every time I walk down the street."

Everybody laughed. Everybody was getting happier. It was like an innocent, childish game. He wanted to make everybody as happy as possible. A lovely looking lady with iron-gray hair and a cheerful face was beckoning him. She was Miss Taylor, the beauty specialist. He really wanted to sit with her.

"You probably feel we're all pretty stupid, don't you?" she asked.

"Lord, no, lady, why should I?" he said.

She looked charming because she was a little ashamed. Rubbing one of her polished nails with the tip of a finger, and watching him with her bright, black eyes, she said, "It's just stupid curiosity, I know. Curiosity is a terrible thing. It gets in you bit by bit. I'm a terribly curious person. I ask the most shameless questions."

"You've got to have curiosity. I'd still be a bandit, wouldn't I, if my curiosity hadn't led me on to ask all these questions?"

"I've never been able to figure out why you never killed anybody."

"I can't say as I ever sat down and thought about it, lady."

"You never wanted to kill anybody at all?"

"Wait a minute. Did you ever feel like killing anybody?"

She laughed and said, "Of course I have. I've got a terrible temper, simply terrible. All my life I've had to keep the brakes on. But you were coasting free, no brakes at all, and you let them catch you rather than kill a man. Why?"

Looking around at all the people he said, slowly, "I figure it was because I liked people too much. I think I always liked all kinds of people. That's all I know."

"You sound so awfully innocent," she said. "It sounds funny coming from you in this place."

"Sure – innocent – that's what I want," he said earnestly.

"A guy like me's had a lot of time to figure these things out. Here's what I mean, lady," he said. "A guy, when he's a little kid, is innocent about things, see? The world looks pretty fresh to him – well, you go on and get smart about it all, and everything's no good. You can't help it. And most people stop right there. But a guy can go on a lot further, he can go right through that phony wise guy stuff he picked up cheap, see? And if you get really smart about the world in a big way you get kind of innocent again, see?"

Eleven

B<small>UT SOMEONE</small> was calling, "Kip, oh, Kip," a voice calling out of his old life. He got up slowly. "Excuse me," he said to the lady. A few tables away was Joe Foley, the little fur thief who had worked with him in the penitentiary shoe shop at the time he had begun his reformation. He was sitting with a squat bald-headed burglar named Ike Kerrmann.

As soon as Kip got close to them Foley began to snicker, starting in where he left off five years ago. His thick glasses shone in the light as he brushed away the strands of black hair that fell into his eyes. Both Foley and Kerrmann looked grotesque in their rented dinner jackets. Foley's shoulders were covered with dandruff. He was the only convict Kip had known who did not have a special break in his character, like Louie the big Negro, who was mild and quiet when no little girls were around, or like the little Limey who was all right except that he liked corpses. Foley was always proudly the one integrated thing, himself.

"Shake pal, you worked it," Foley said.

"Worked what?"

"This thing you started when I was down there with you."

"What thing?"

"Come on, drop it; you don't need to keep it up with me," Foley said, snickering. They looked at each other and there was no use saying anything. Five years ago in the prison Foley used to put his forefinger on top of his head and spin round under it like a top whenever he heard Kip giving advice to a green kid to go straight.

"My God, you're in the big time now," Kerrmann whispered. He was awed. "There's a lot of heavy sugar here. What a fancy set-up!"

"What's the set-up?" Foley whispered.

"Just what it looks like," Kip said, smiling.

"You mean you're just fronting around here? Just a gold fish for these mugs?" Foley had a sleepy, purring voice. As he grinned the light shone on his bad lower teeth. "You're wonderful. You got a talent, brother," he said. His dark face was full of admiration. "You got the whole town wide open. We can do big things with this, you and me."

"Don't be a chump, Joe," Kip said, laughing at him.

"Me a chump? Go on, take the grin off your big stupid face. The town pet, eh! Is some fat old millionaire's wife teaching you parlor tricks? What are you going to do? Stand up now and say your prayers for these rich mugs?"

While Foley went on yapping at him, he stared into his quivering, bad-tempered face. It wasn't like Kerrmann's face. Kerrmann was a slow-witted man who never had any education and had grown up in reform schools. Foley, of poor Irish people in Chicago, had been given some education, but it had only separated him from his people. He hated them; they were slobs. He hated their superstitions, their aspirations, their faith that he felt had marked him forever. And all smooth-mannered rich people he hated because he never could be like them.

"Remember the time you and me escaped, Foley?" Kip said. "Remember how we came down the road in the mud and you dropped your glasses and fell and I put you on my shoulders and you let me carry you along a mile, thinking you were hurt? In those days I was the patsy for you."

"Aw, bull, bull. You got out. There was only one train to town for you and you took it. You got off the train as soon as it got this far, see. Don't you think it hasn't occurred to anybody?"

Looking around at the people who kept watching them Kip longed to know what they were thinking. "Take it from me, everybody here's thinking the same thing," Foley said. But voices were still calling, "When you've got a minute, Kip," and "When you're passing this way, Kip –" Friendly voices calling him away from Foley's life. "You're crazy, Foley," he whispered.

Suddenly whistles started to blow; everybody was screaming, and Kip jumped, bewildered, towering among them. Colored balloons soared to the ceiling, everybody threw paper streamers that fell over his shoulders, while people embraced, girls kissed their lovers, and horns blared and rattles clack clacked. "Happy New Year, happy New New Year," they screamed.

"Jesus," he said. "I didn't know what it was for a minute." Grabbing a horn, he started blowing it. He was waving the horn madly over his head, yelling "Happy New Year everybody," when Jenkins pushed his way through the mob and grabbed him.

"Come on, now's the time," he said.

"So long, Joe," Kip yelled.

"So long nothing," Foley yelled. "We got a date."

Jenkins led him up to the orchestra platform, and there they stood watching the crowd milling around. The boy rolled the drums; they put a spotlight on Jenkins and he held up his hand for silence.

"Ladies and gentlemen," he shouted. "There goes the old year and here's the new one knocking on the door. I'm wishing you all lots of luck and happy days. But the best thing about it is from this minute on we all get a fresh start, we quit beefing and take a fresh toehold and feel we got another big chance to lead the league in something. If it was tough for us, we've got a chance to make it different. No matter how good it was, it can be a lot better. We've all got our hearts full of good resolutions, God bless us. We couldn't live if we didn't have them. And this is a night you're going to remember because we've got some-one here with us ..." He was turning slowly and pointing at Kip who was just touched by the fringe of the spotlight ... "Someone who stands for all the good resolutions we ever made. And I'm here saying happy New Year, Kip. What do you say?"

As the spotlight fell on Kip he was standing with his head down, his hands clenched tight in front of him, scared that someone would laugh. Blinking his eyes, he looked all around; then he raised both his hands. There was a wonderfully spon-taneous burst of applause, then silence. A young voice called "Okay, Kip." Someone said a little brokenly, "Good luck to you." He knew how truly moved they were. He let his hands drop slowly to his sides. He seemed to become the prodigal son of the whole country. The faces close to him blurred. He saw Connick's face, and a thousand others like his all brightening with hope.

"Speech, speech," somebody shouted. He wanted to tell them of the work he dreamed of doing, but he was nervous.

"Give us a speech," they shouted.

"Not me," he said humbly.

They were crazy with curiosity to have him make a speech. "Come on, Kip, speech, speech, say something," they shouted.

Jerking his head back, he said, "Sure – I'd like to say some-thing. But just this – I wanted you to forget me – I wanted to forget myself. The way you've welcomed me was worth wait-ing for a long time. I don't care if nothing else ever happens to me. I never saw most of you in my life, but this is the one night in my life I want to remember. This welcome. No one who ever went away got a better hand. I hope we always have this good feeling – It's all you can ask– It's the best thing in the world –

and well – many thanks and a happy New Year to you all," and he backed out of the spotlight, wiped his face with his handkerchief and wondered why they were all so quiet.

"Hurrah for Kip," somebody shouted.

"Hurrah for Caley."

"Hurrah, hurrah," they shouted. It was his apotheosis.

Twelve

He had to get away from them for a few minutes, so deeply was he moved. He was hurrying out when he saw someone waving to him from the door. It was the big raw-boned, red-headed priest, Father Butler. It seemed beautiful that he had come on such a night. The light was shining on his broad freckled face as he leaned against the hat-check counter. The little check girl was kidding him, for his heavy, fur-collared coat, high around his neck concealed his Roman collar. "This is wonderful," Kip said when he got close to him. "What a happy New Year!"

"Maybe it was the wrong night for me to come," Father Butler said. Kip saw that he looked unhappy – the first unhappy-looking face Kip had seen that night.

"What are you looking sad about?" he asked.

"Maybe it is a look I get on my face when I come into the city," Father Butler said. But he didn't believe him; he didn't believe anybody was unhappy.

He felt so buoyant, the priest began to laugh too. They linked arms and went up to Kip's room. He phoned for a drink for the priest, asked him where he was staying, begged him to stay the night there with him; he himself could sleep on the couch. There were so many things they had to talk about. There were questions he wanted to ask about the prison and the convicts who were his friends. And most of all he wanted to know what the priest thought of his job and the reception they had given him.

"I never dreamed it would happen," he said.

"Did you see it, did you hear it?"

"You're their miracle," the priest said, smiling.

"Honest – were you there?"

The priest was taking off his coat and undoing his collar. "I just saw the end of it," he said. Looking around the room, he said, "Have you got a pair of slippers?"

"Mine," he said, getting them. And he stood there remembering. "They had me mixed up for a while."

"The Senator is here too, eh?"

"He's a prince! Not just to me either. They tell me he's given hundreds of thousands of dollars to charities."

"Such munificence is usually a sure sign of a love of power," the priest said dryly. He was putting on the slippers and he didn't look up. "Oh, sure, he's a fine fellow," he said. "I was a little surprised to see him here looking so happy. He was pretty worried the last time I saw him." Sighing, he stretched out his slippered feet. "That's better, much better," he said. And then he smiled. "I saw Jenkins downstairs. He has an extraordinary face – every line of it, what is it?"

Kip smiled at him and nodded, remembering Jenkins' beautiful speech. He wanted to lie down with his old friend there in the room, and just breathe and feel the quickening in all things.

"You feel pretty good, don't you?" the priest said.

"Just happy, that's all."

"I've never seen you look so happy."

"Why don't you look happy?"

"I was just thinking."

"I know what you're thinking."

The priest hesitated, troubled. "I was just wondering what this means – what you are heading for. Where are you going?"

"Where am I going? I've got a lot of plans – big plans – to tell you," he said. But then they heard a crowd from the dance hall on the corner rushing out on the street, shouting "Auld Lang Syne," their voices wild. He stood with the priest at the window. They saw the group coming from the dance hall, their faces raised, the snow pouring down on their faces as they sang. They swayed drunkenly and pushed each other around and finally tumbled, whooping in the big snowpile, screaming at each other: "Happy New Year. Happy New Year."

"It all sounds sort of innocent and grand, like listening to a bunch of kids. When you get them like that they'll give you anything," Kip said.

"If the gifts are good …"

"What?"

"Have you heard of the gifts that destroy?"

"Then you're disappointed," Kip said. But any kind of disappointment seemed unreal on such a night. It didn't touch him at all. With the new year flowing in on them, with the snow drifting across the street lights, making the earth freshly white for the new year, he wanted to keep his joy unspoiled.

"I wonder if it's snowing down at the prison," the priest said.

"Was it when you left?"

"I understand it is snowing all over tonight," he said.

They heard the laughter again from the streets, the music from downstairs. The priest watched those heavy flakes of snow streaming down in the dark night; they seemed to draw him away alone. In spite of his joy, Kip's memory of things was with the priest's out there where the white snow fell in the dark. They were like the two men on the journey again, meeting after they had gone on a little farther.

"They talk a lot about you in the prison," the priest said. "I don't know one of them that doesn't wish you luck; I don't know one that doesn't seem to have a little more hope of getting out. They figure that if it worked for you it can work for any one of them. So you see, Kip, you're on that white horse."

"Only I'm not by myself now."

"That's right. There's a long parade behind you."

"All the jailbirds in the country."

"Every one who figures he isn't going to be given a chance."

It touched Kip's dream. His eyes shone and he said eagerly, "I'm going to stay with them out here like I did down there – I want to get on the parole board." Then he told the priest how he had got the idea. He told him how Steve Connick had died; he reminded him how successfully he had worked with the men in prison. Even the Mayor had invited him to see him and talk about prison conditions; maybe it was necessary that the priest speak to the Senator about it. "You've always listened to me. Do you know anybody who could do such work better?" he said.

"You'd bring great understanding to it, but how could you get it?"

"Like I said. You tell the Senator how good I'd be at it. He's got all kinds of influence."

"You're forgetting something – Judge Ford is on the parole board."

"I know."

"Judge Ford didn't want to let you out."

"That's all right. That was before I came out," Kip said, and he laughed confidently.

"All right – I'll speak to the Senator," the priest said, but he sighed. "But I know you won't come back now," he said.

"Back!"

"I came here to ask you to come back and be my gardener – maybe for a year till people get used to you being free."

Kip knew the priest was pleading with him, and he was astonished. He looked out at the freshly white street, remembering the spontaneous applause and how moved everybody had been. His eyes were shining as he shook his head at the priest. "No – no," he said softly. "Listen, what would you have thought of the prodigal son if he had come home, and found his old man and his family had got a big feast ready and invited all the neighbors in and they were all getting ready for a swell time, and the son takes one look at them and refuses to sit down on account of them wanting to make a fuss over him? What would you have thought of him? They have to call it all off because he's feeling sour. A killjoy – too dumb and self-centered to see it didn't mean anything, unless he met them half way. Is it going to be that way with me?"

"How odd!"

"Why?"

"That you should have figured it out." The priest rubbed the side of his slipper on the rug and pondered. "That's quite an idea. Maybe the prodigal son had a job going from feast to feast till the end of his days. Maybe anybody who wanted an excuse to have a feast invited him out; maybe he had a job at it for the rest of his life. I wonder what happened to him after the feasting was over."

Thirteen

JUDGE FORD who had sentenced Kip to life and twenty lashes was standing across the road from the hotel one night in the shelter of the grocery-store door out of the glare of the big red Coronet light. He had a touch of bronchitis, but he stood there in the snow.

Everybody knew he had opposed Kip's parole. Whenever he went to his club for lunch some younger member asked him slyly if he had been reading Kip's life story in the papers. But he only laughed good-humoredly. At four o'clock in the afternoon when he came walking down the city hall steps, a tall, erect, very clean-looking man, his white beard shining in the afternoon sun, he could tell if there was another big picture of Kip by the way the newsboy hesitated handing him his paper. The latest picture had shown Kip leaning against the car the G. & W. Motor Company had sold him. A week ago he had seen Kip walking lazily along the city hall corridor with Mayor Wills, laughing as if he owned the place. And the other day a brother judge, amiable, sentimental old Hubert Mackenzie, had asked Kip to sit on the bench with him.

When the Judge came to his office in the mornings before court opened he used to toss his newspaper at his stenographer and laugh, "Caley's talking about the care and feeding of convicts now. But I suppose people have to have some kind of a hero," he said indulgently. "They get the kind of hero their time deserves." Looking grave, he added, "But it's moral bankruptcy just the same."

The Judge wasn't a malicious man. He came of a fine, important family. His father, one of the town's great merchants had owned a department store and sold it and founded a trust company. The Judge hoped Kip would keep out of trouble. But from all he knew of him he believed him to be essentially lawless and violent. And when he heard that Senator Maclean, women's clubs, and the Mayor had suggested that Kip be given a position on the parole board it seemed to him to be a mockery of the law and order he loved above everything.

Day after day, on the bench in court, as he stared into the faces of old criminals, he remembered that time ten years ago when Caley had shouted at him: "I'm different. I'm not like you," and they had grabbed him and pulled him away shouting. He began to ask himself what it was in Caley that stirred people. The shifty-eyed prisoners were frightened by his deliberate interest in them. Yet he was only wondering if any one of them might be able to stir up people as Kip had done. His curiosity to see Kip developed like a secret passion, but of course he had no intention of yielding to it.

That night he stood outside the hotel, he had told his wife he was only going out for a walk, but he found himself standing watching people going in and out of the Coronet. "It couldn't have happened twenty years ago. People have softened up terribly. Look at them going in – young people, all young people going to gape at a convict and watch him grin. Do they want to touch him? Good God, look at those girls. Look at the way they laugh. Maybe they're drunk. They surely can't believe in anything!" he thought. But he crossed the road himself, walked by the big blue-coated doorman, entered the door, and stood listening. He started to walk away and stopped. "I'm a little chilled. Maybe I should warm myself," he thought, and he came back slowly. Then he went on past the doorman again. He stood near the light, telling himself to go on home. "I refused to agree to his parole. Maybe it's my duty to see what he's doing in there," he thought. He became like a child; he was walking slowly by the entrance again. The doorman touched his hat to him this time and he stopped struggling and went in.

When the pert-nosed, blonde, little hat-check girl called: "Check your coat, sir?" he turned, startled, then he bowed to her. "No, no, never mind, thank you." he said.

Near the door was a table by a palm tree and he sat down, sure that no one had noticed him. He ordered a whiskey and soda. Out on the floor they were dancing, a Negro was playing the saxophone; he heard the high-pitched voices of women. And then out of the hum of conversation and laughter he heard one low, rumbling, eager voice. Leaning out from behind the palm he saw Kip sitting at a table with two young lads who looked like college boys. Kip's face looked just as bold and wild as it did that day ten years ago, except that it now had an expression of deep security. His shoulders looked enormous. He was telling a story and waving his arms, watching the serious faces of the lads light up, looking like a mariner back from a new world, regaling children with tales of his adventures.

"What's he talking about? Why do they look like that when they listen? If I could just hear a bit of it I'd go. I ought to know what he's doing here," the Judge said to himself. He swung his chair out from the table, and leaned toward Kip, listening. And Kip, waving his arm, turned, then dropped the arm slowly, and the Judge knew he had seen him.

The Judge gulped down his whiskey, and got up and started to go, with Kip hurrying after him. Then the Judge was ashamed; he felt he had been just as curious, just as fascinated

as any high-school boy. He had let his dreadful curiosity muti-
late his spirit. But he turned near the checkroom, and waited,
a little flushed but smiling.

"Why didn't you let me know you were coming?" Kip said,
his hand out. The Judge's dignity seemed to impress him
deeply. "It means a great deal to me to have you come here to
see me," he said.

"There was a friend out this way," the Judge began.
Ashamed of the lie, he said, "I had some interest in your case,
Caley. I had a strong opinion, as everybody knows. I have an
interest in you."

"That is what I want," Kip said. He was staring at the
Judge's white head, his white beard, and the big white cuffs
that seemed to make his hands seem old. "Gee, the years certainly slipped by, didn't they? But I knew you as soon as I saw
you," he said.

Anxious to take a little thrust that might stir Kip into
betraying himself, the Judge said, smiling, "Yes, the years
slipped by, and now they've set you to music."

"That's all right, Judge. I want to talk to you – about the
parole board …"

"This is hardly the place."

"Don't go. You've got me all wrong. Why can't you feel
friendly?" Kip said, grabbing his arm.

"I've got nothing against you, only I don't think you should
be here like this," the Judge said. Then he remembered that his
own shameful curiosity had brought him here. "God only
knows why we're all so curious," he said.

"Maybe there's another way of looking at it," Kip said.
"What's wrong with people liking to have a guy around that
gives them a good feeling? You ought to stay around here for a
while and see what I mean." His voice became slow and
dreamy. "It's hard figuring it out, and I'd like to get your angle
on it. I've been thinking there's been hundreds of guys like me

in the world. Something happens – it's like a spark – it touches people – and it's a great thing for everybody."

The Judge was astonished. While Kip was speaking, he kept watching the dreamy smile on his big dark face. But when he had finished the spell was broken. The Judge pulled away from him.

"You believe this?" he said.

"Sure."

"A bubble a boy blows out of a clay pipe," the Judge whispered.

"What?"

"You must be a little crazy."

"Me crazy?" he asked, and he let out a burst of good-humored laughter.

"My God, this crazy demoralizing kind of grandeur, he really believes it," the Judge said. He was shocked and he hurried out.

Fourteen

W HEN KIP went back to the table where the two university boys were waiting, he was very happy. "This is wonderful. Maybe the Judge knows he's going to have to play ball with the Senator. Maybe they had a talk today," he thought. The Senator, who had been out of the city, had returned two days ago, and Kip was waiting to hear from him.

"Who was that?" one of the students asked.

"Judge Ford."

"What did he want?"

"I don't know, unless it was to see how I was doing. The main thing is he came; that's terribly important," he said. He smiled at the boys' serious faces, feeling that same dreamy exaltation. "What was I saying when the Judge came in?"

"About big Louie."

"Sure, Louie, I can see him the day he came, nearly seven feet tall, a great big powerful buck Negro sent down for life and you wouldn't want to touch him. Nobody would speak to him. The great big whopper had gone after a little girl and used a knife on her." Raising both hands he leaned close to them but his voice wasn't vibrant and his face didn't glow because he was still really thinking of the Judge. "Louie had a big lovely grin. It was like a kid's grin. The first time he flashed it a little guy spit at him and I had to grab Louie and nearly break his arm. I tried to tell him it wouldn't go. Look what I'm getting at! There were no little girls down there and Louie had to be like you and me, just a single guy in a big wide world. He had to forget what his weakness was. Even the guards had to forget it. He does little favors for them like shining their shoes, and the big ape can tap dance too."

Smiling with his eyes half closed he was looking beyond them, thinking of Louie. Then he suddenly saw her. She was coming in, looking all around with that candid childlike expression on her face. Whispering "Excuse me" to the boys he stood up, watching her. Like someone waiting in a crowd and worrying she looked at the three hockey players, at the table near her. The Negro at the drums smiled at her. And then she saw him. Her face shone; she waved her brown gloved hand.

"Julie – I didn't think you'd come," he said.

"Why?"

Maybe his beating heart and his wonder made him look strange to her, because she hesitated, holding her purse in both her hands, her face flushed.

"I don't know. Maybe because I wanted you to," he said. His surprise seemed to please her.

"I had to see the shoemaker," she said. She kept watching him as if making sure he was like the picture of him she kept in her head. She had on a new brown coat, a brown felt hat, and a high red-necked sweater. In a way she looked to be very simply and carelessly dressed, yet the hockey players were staring at her as if they were seeing such clothes for the first time.

"You look different. Last time I saw you, you looked ready for the cleaners," he said. "What happened? Come on. Sit down and tell me. Have something to drink."

"A little rum with pineapple juice," she said. "It never leaves me with a headache." Then she smiled and put out her hand to him. "Thanks for the galoshes, and the shoes," she said.

"I was scared you'd find out who I was," he said, worried a little.

"Isn't it funny?"

"What?"

"We talk as if we'd known each other a long time."

"It's the way I feel."

"I'm modeling again. You made me come alive that night."

It seemed a wonderful thing for her to say. He wanted to tell her how important she had been to him.

"Whenever I see somebody that reminds me of that night with you a part of me that is still hard and stiff is broken and everything comes flowing in light and warm. See what I mean?"

"Why, that's beautiful," she said.

"It's what I mean," he said.

But people who were staring at them bothered her. "What do you really do here?" she asked.

"Oh, just try and see everybody has a good time."

"Is that all?"

"Why?"

"The thing you have – do they understand? You have integrity," she said. Her face was glowing. She was offering him a kind of respect that was new to him.

"I'm not just sitting around here," he said. "Jenkins has been burning up about it. But I'm here working on a big thing – an awful big thing. I'm trying to get on the parole board." He wanted it to delight her; he wanted to show her now how the world was widening out for him. "You know who was here a little while ago? Judge Ford! He came to see me. You can see why. I may be working with him. Didn't you see that picture they took of me at the police benefit concert?"

"No," she said. "I wish I had."

"It was in all the papers. Where have you been? Come on into the bar. It's hanging on the wall there, I'll show it to you," he said, slipping his arm around her. He led her among the tables, bowing to people as he passed. A beautiful red-headed girl from the West, with a milky skin, who was going upstairs with two men, blew him a kiss off her hand.

"Who's that?" Julie said

"Oh, that's May Hamilton. I was out with her last night," he said.

They stood together at the bar, looking at the enlarged photograph hanging over the big bowl of lemons, the pretzel bowl and the row of glasses. It showed him smiling broadly and shaking hands with Police Chief Symonds and Mayor Wills, with a background of four police inspectors, all smiling eagerly at the camera. "That's the Chief," he said, pointing. "The one with the big moustache – hard-headed and a little grumpy and self-important but a great guy. It was a swell concert. We had some vaudeville stars there. I made a little speech about the attitude a cop ought to take to a paroled man. I certainly had them feeling it could all be so damn different. I had them thinking and feeling like a thousand jailbirds think and feel." As he gripped the edge of the bar his eyes were shining.

He tried to take her into those days and nights around town – the big parties, the studious little groups, then sitting in Mayor Wills' office, going everywhere with friendly laughter, into fine discussions about prisons that lasted till dawn. They kept coming from far away, a stream of eager faces flowing past him in the hotel, too many to remember, doctors, lawyers, clergymen, and the publisher who came and got him to sign a contract to write a book. Each night widened it out further; hockey games with the Macleans, the fight crowds, that fine night they introduced him from the ring and he shook hands with the two lightweights; that night he got sore at the man from the insurance company and the automobile salesman who offered him jobs. "That was different," he said. "It had no dignity."

"No," she said. "You couldn't do that."

Then Eddie, the red-headed bartender called, "The phone for you, Kip. Take it here?"

"Now you stay right here. Don't go away," he said to her anxiously. When he went to the phone at the end of the bar and heard the Senator's voice he said excitedly, "What is it? Some news?"

"Why don't you come up and see me tomorrow night?" the Senator said.

"I'd love to."

"A few people will be there. A white tie, eh?"

"Fine. You're sure there's nothing new about the parole board?"

"We'll go into it then," the Senator said.

Then Kip went back to Julie. He squeezed her arm almost boyishly. "That was the Senator," he said. "We're going to get this thing all fixed up. Come on, let me walk home with you."

It was a strange moment while she hesitated; but he had his hand on her arm, pulling her to him.

"All right, come on," she said.

He got his hat and coat, and it was a Saturday evening and little crowds of loafers were hanging around the front of the hotel, one of those winter evenings when everybody seems soft and white and you imagine a green spring is on the way. "Hello, Kip," they called. "How ya, how ya, everybody?" he said. He held her arm close to him; he felt her fervor and faith. It brought him joy. He told her how he wanted to be a link between the two worlds, the outcasts and the right-thinking people. The lace on her galoshes came undone and he knelt down in the snow and tied it for her, his face raised, talking all the time. "You say I'm just sitting around there, don't you," he said. "But already a lot of old jailbirds have started coming to me for advice and I talk with the cops about them. See?"

"Ouch, you tied it too tight," she said.

Kneeling in the snow, holding her foot in his hand, he looked up at her and said suddenly, "Say, what about you?"

"What about me?"

"Where are you from?"

"A place in the country and a place in the city."

"You're kidding me."

"My father lived part of the year in Pennsylvania near Delaware. He was a building contractor. My mother married a druggist and lived in Buffalo."

"Then how did you get here?"

"I ran away."

"Why?"

She said she was shuffled back and forth between two homes since her parents parted when she was eight, and she was a stranger in each home. There were other children. When her mother came one day to the Pennsylvania place to get her, she heard them quarreling. She realized that for years neither one of them really wanted her. One took her to spite the other. Looking up at her, he shook his head.

"They must have been snow-blind," he said. Then his knee felt wet and he finished tying the knot and got up and brushed the snow off his knee. "Go on, why are you stopping?" he said.

"I ran away that night," she said, "but they brought me back. I stayed around a few years, keeping to myself and I used to go up on the hill a lot and look across the Delaware to the Jersey hills and pretend it was another country. I used to dress up and pretend I was all the famous women I used to read about. Then I came away and wanted to be a model. But I was just a kid when I started and I was an easy mark for a big talking buyer."

"Don't you ever feel like going home?"

"They write me and I write them sometimes. It's like writing to the dead," she said. "I seem to come of a family that can't help messing things up. That's why it's wonderful you should be able to take your life and make it mean something," she said. "It's heroic."

They walked on through the snow and he was profoundly moved that she had tied her life up with his. When they got to her place he sat down on the green couch while she took off her coat and hat. She offered to scramble some eggs and make him some coffee. She seemed to want to keep him there. He watched her put on a little white apron. While she was breaking the eggs in the pan and getting the cups out of the cupboard he got up and stood by the stove. She kept turning her head, smiling and talking rapidly. When she saw him watching her so seriously, she said, "What's the matter?"

"I was just thinking it didn't feel much like the hotel here," he said.

The sound of the eggs cooking on the pan, the noise the dishes made, her white apron, reminded him of the longing he used to have in prison for a simple life. The room seemed like a home. It was like a new and beautiful thing he had come upon that he wanted to take away with him. And when she was cutting some bread he went over and stood behind her looking down at the black hair on her neck. He put out both his hands, slow and hesitant, to touch her gently. Then she turned. Her eyes widened. She leaned back tense against the edge of the table, looking up at him with her mouth opening.

"What's the matter?" he said, hurt a little.

"Nothing."

"Look at your face. Your eyes are shining and you're trembling."

"Am I?"

"Are you scared of me?"

"No," she whispered. "I don't know what I felt." She was

looking up at him as if he were offering her a dream of a great, surging adventurous life. "I guess I just feel you open everything up for me," she said.

"That's a grand thing for anybody to do," he said. But the feeling that seemed to widen out the world for him almost as much as his parole board dream was the feeling he had standing beside her at the stove.

Fifteen

He went down to Henderson's department store and had lunch there and watched her walking among the tables modeling a white crepe dress. But she didn't see him. That night when he was running down the hotel stairs all dressed up he was still thinking of her. "No so fast, not so fast, mister," Jenkins called from the lobby.

"I was in a hurry."

"Where the hell do you think you're going? People go away if you don't stick around," Jenkins said.

"It can't be crowded all the time," Kip said.

"Why doesn't the Senator bring his crowd around here any more?"

"He's been to a sanatorium taking a liquor cure. I'm going to see him tonight."

"Am I getting a percentage on the Senator's parties?"

"But this is something big. The Parole Board."

"That's no skin on my nose. Stay around here and talk to a few people for a change," Jenkins said sourly. But Kip was too excited to be bothered with him. He got a cab, and drove by Julie's place. When he discovered she wasn't in, he waited around a while and saw her coming along the street slowly, her coat open. Running to her, he grabbed her and rushed her into

94

the cab. "I had to see you, kid. Come on, ride over with me to the Senator's place," he said.

"You just about knocked my hat off."

"I like it like that."

"I'm out of breath," she laughed. "It's like catching a train."

"Going where?"

"Right to the end of the line."

"And going fast."

"Phone me as soon as you hear anything definite."

"It may be very late, kid."

"I'll be waiting. I'll listen to the radio all night," she said. "Promise me, please, promise me." Her face was lifted up to him.

He felt her breathless eagerness to share his life. It awed him. "Well, gee whiz," he said. Everything seemed to be widening out further and further. "Why, sure, kid," he said, as the lurching cab threw her against him. "I'll let you know first thing."

In front of the Senator's house there were cars lined far along the curb. When Julie, in their cab, passed beyond the street light, he still kept the brightness of her hope for him. Now he was not only famous and important to people, he was in love, and he was loved. Those lighted windows in the Senator's big house reminded him of the first night he had come home and had looked at the sweep of lights across the river. "Look how far I've gone in such a little while," he said to himself. His childhood, the poverty of his mother's home, the pool parlors, the prison years had led unbelievably to this great house. "And I thought one time I'd never be able to make the grade! What'll I talk about? I'll stick to the things I know something about. I won't take a long lead and get caught off the bag. I won't argue with them. These big people mightn't like it," he thought, going up to the door.

When the butler let him in, the Senator's wife, a big lumpy

woman, who had been married for her money, and who hardly ever appeared publicly with the Senator, met him in the hall and said vaguely, "Mr. Caley, oh, yes, Mr. Caley." She seemed to be completely separated from the Senator's life. Laughing, he put his arm on her shoulder. "It's swell to see you, Mrs. Maclean," he said. She was startled. But he made her feel important in her own home.

He went into the drawing room with her and didn't notice how the chatter stopped. He was looking around for the Senator in the gathering of brokers, financial men and their wives and a few professors. When Ellen came to him with her hands out, blonde and sleek all in white, he followed her eagerly to the people she said were dying to meet him, the people, he thought who should hear his ideas about the parole system and prison conditions.

He got right behind General Crighton, and Mrs. Mactavish, a broker's wife with a diamond tiara in her hair, before they noticed him. "Oh, oh," she cried, her fingers on her mouth.

"What's the matter, lady?" he asked, startled himself.

"Well, looking up, seeing you standing there," she said, fluttering.

But the General, a vain, spoiled, rich man, hardly paused. "Yes, as I was saying. At lunch yesterday with Lord Standish, passing through on his way to the coast, he assured me there would be no war for at least two years." Yet he kept looking at Kip out of the corner of his eye, as if he were duelling with him, thinking, "I'm the important one here."

"That's mighty interesting, General," Kip said. He couldn't feel insulted, for groups of people were hurrying over to him, the first one among them the General's own wife, a bright-eyed, plump woman. He liked the way they all bowed to him. He liked their soft voices, but he wondered why the General's wife kept whispering to one of the professors.

"We were wondering about prison life," the professor said.

"I'd be glad to talk about it from any angle," he said, very pleased.

"About the life there, the – um, um, shall we say, depriva-tions …"

"Deprivations? What are you getting at?"

Everybody was smiling, and he was embarrassed because he didn't know what they were talking about.

"After all, they're all men – and confined and they have hungers, haven't they?" the professor said.

"They certainly have."

"The unsatisfied hungers … Well, sex, for instance," the General's wife said, shrugging and smiling.

"Oh, that! I see," Kip said. "Why, gee!" He was very disap-pointed. He had no heart for a discussion of sexual perver-sions, which might cheapen him in the eyes of these people he thought so important. He kept looking around restlessly for the Senator; then his face brightened. He saw him coming in. He tried to get a glimpse of the expression on the Senator's face, as if it could tell him if his hope was fulfilled. "Excuse me," he said. He left them heading for the Senator.

"What about it?" he whispered when he was close to him.

"About what?"

"The parole board – where do I stand?"

"Aren't you drinking anything? Come on and we'll have a drink and chat," the Senator said. He led him across the hall and up the wide stairs to the oak-paneled library.

"Come on – what's the news? What chance have I got?" Kip said.

Pondering, the Senator began to walk up and down on the bright red carpet. "It's going to be difficult, I'm afraid – just about as difficult as it could be."

"You don't mean …"

"What?"

"There's no chance?" Kip said.

"Here's the situation. Judge Ford says he'll resign and make a public issue of it. That would be dangerous, dangerous for all of us, you understand. There'd be a hell of a scandal," he said, but he looked unhappy, as if Kip, there in his house with his life widening, had made him feel for a while like a creator – a feeling he had to have, and which he had also felt last week when a man came to him with a plan for getting eighty miles an hour out of a gallon of gasoline, a boon to millions of people.

"I could try and push this thing through," he said. "I believe with all my heart you'd do a great work on that parole board, but look, Kip – it would be political suicide."

"You'd let a hard guy like the Judge put you off?" Kip said.

"I find there's a line-up against me. It would have to be fought in the open. What can I do?"

"We'll fight it in the open – it's a big thing, isn't it? Everybody would be behind us."

"I'm sorry, but I don't think so."

"You mean you'd let that guy ring the bell on you," Kip said. The Senator seemed like a little boy who had let go a toy balloon to see how high it would rise, and then watched it drift out of sight.

Kip sat rubbing the sole of his shoe on the rug; then he looked up, unbelieving, as if he had just realized what this meant. It wasn't just the job; it was a part of life that was being denied him, the aspirations of a free man. "Senator," he begged him, "you aren't going to take this, are you?"

"What I want is one thing …" the Senator began.

"I'm surprised, Senator, terribly surprised," he said. "I don't mean that – you've been generous – it's not you …" He went over to the window and looked over the city that sloped from the hill down to the lake. He felt he loved it. He wanted the fullness of its life – to be able to reach out and touch the fine thing his talent might lead him to. There were circles of light over high buildings, and great dark shadowy valleys where there were low unlighted buildings, and behind the valleys were clusters of illuminated towers. In those streets down there he had walked with Julie, thinking everything was close to him. It shone like a magic city, and the Judge, he felt, would segregate him from all the responsible places.

Stuttering a little, he said, "Why, the Judge came to see me just like anybody else. The Judge and me ought to take a good look at each other – have a talk – see what makes us tick like we do. Why, say, maybe he'd find out that the things he thinks are so big and important are the things I think too. What do you say?" he pleaded.

"Of course, if you can win the Judge over," the Senator said. Shrugging, he flicked his cigar. "That's another thing," he said.

"But you don't feel licked, do you?"

"In these matters you're never licked," the Senator said. "It's like drilling for gold. If it's not there you try some other place – It's not a personal defeat." He squeezed Kip's arm. "Come on, have a cigar and we'll go downstairs."

The Senator was so bland and so firmly established in his own big world, it made Kip feel all the more insecure. He couldn't say anything to him going downstairs. He was thinking of the Judge, still thinking how he had come to see him just like anybody else, hearing himself talking to him, and he didn't see Ellen standing alone in the hall waiting for them.

"Hello," she called. "I thought you'd gone for the evening." She stood there, smiling up at him. The Senator, giving him a pat on the shoulder and a grave smile, walked on alone with the light shining on his red neck and fine white head.

"Do you want to go in there and answer their silly questions?" she asked him.

"I don't care one way or the other," he said. He didn't feel like talking to anybody but the Judge.

"Don't I ever get a chance to talk to you alone?"

"If you want to," he said, lifelessly. As she led him into the conservatory he wasn't paying much attention to her. Her interest in him seemed unimportant. It seemed like the interest of a little girl fluttering around a celebrity. They sat down, Ellen leaning close to him.

"I was bored," she sighed. "I've been bored for weeks."

"What?"

"Just bored – but not now."

"I don't feel much like giving anybody a lift," he said, thinking of the Judge.

"What do you mean?"

"If you want someone to set you up …"

"Is that nice?"

"I don't feel like it, that's all."

"What's the matter with you?"

"What about those gents in the other room …"

"No, thanks," she said, "I've got a mink coat," and she screwed up her eyes so the little wrinkles were at the corners, the shape of her breasts showing in her white dress. But he was impatient with her; he thought he could scare her away. Grabbing her, he pulled her against him and held her. But she didn't struggle, she lay against him, her heart beating against him, yielding to him. He was dreadfully surprised. She had seemed beyond him; he could have her if he wanted her. All his hopefulness rose again and with it a surge of power. He wanted to rush out right then and see Judge Ford.

Sixteen

WHEN HE got back to the hotel he couldn't go to bed. He sat in a chair by the window for hours, making little speeches, opening his life to the Judge. When he got undressed, he lay wide awake staring at the patch of moonlight on the mound his feet made under the covers. He wondered if Julie was still listening to the radio, waiting. He got up and walked around in his bare feet. It seemed to him that there in that room in the moonlight he and the Judge met and the Judge became very friendly and said some fine things. Outside all the city birds began a steady cheeping and then it was dawn. He didn't know what time it was when he fell asleep but it was afternoon when he woke up.

When he was passing the desk, Billie called. "That little guy with the glasses and the dandruff was in here looking for you. What's his name?"

"Foley."

"Yeah, Foley. He was in here last night too. What'll I tell him?"

"Tell him I had to go over to the city hall and see a Judge," he said. He got his car, drove over to the city hall, parked across the street from the burlesque show and came across by the cenotaph. There he stood taking a deep breath, looking up the flight of steps to the city hall door. He had gone through that door many times when he was a kid being taken to the juvenile court. He ran up the steps and strode along the corridor and rapped on Judge Ford's door. When the Judge called, "Come in," he steadied himself. The Judge was sitting at his desk by the window overlooking the court yard. He was wiping his glasses with his handkerchief. A stream of sunlight from the high window touched the back of his white head and the blotter on his desk. His face was in the shadow. In the light his shrewd gray eyes seemed to brighten. Standing up slowly, he said, "Good morning, Caley. A return visit, I see."

"Yeah. I wanted to have a little talk," Kip said.

"I see."

"Just a talk," Kip said, hoping the Judge would feel how much he wanted his friendship. The Judge smiled, waiting, and he suddenly felt very hopeful.

"I figured you had, see – something against me – on account of you not wanting them to let me out and on account of this – well – it gives a guy a bad feeling going around, thinking someone like you – someone you'd like to be friendly with has got the thumb on you," he said.

"I've got nothing against you personally, Caley," the Judge said mildly. "It's true I didn't think they ought to let you out, but that's because I felt you'd been violent and lawless all your life."

"I'm not holding that against you," Kip said. "But whatever I've been – there are some things I know something about. This parole board can be a big thing."

"It ought to be. That's right."

"I can do things with people. I can get close to them."

"You know I'm on the board, don't you?"

"Sure. That means I'm aiming pretty high, but ..."

"No, Caley, no," the Judge said, smiling as if he pitied him.

"Look, Judge, a guy like me ..."

"The night I went to see you I thought you were a little

drunk," the Judge said softly. "Look at the terrible thing they've done to you. You've lost all sense of proportion. Look, Caley," he went on gently. "Don't let them do this to you."

"Judge – Judge," he pleaded with him. "You're not talking to me – you're talking to the part of me that is dead – I wish you knew me – I wish we knew each other."

"Maybe we don't," the Judge said. "That's why you think I'm not being just to you. That's what you'll say …"

"Who's worrying about justice?" Kip said. The Judge's voice was soft and patient and he thought he was going to have a chance with him. He was going closer to him, ready to offer him all his eagerness and tell him he only wanted to feel he had a chance at a full life like anybody else, when the door opened. Mayor Wills, carrying a sheaf of papers, came in with his short quick steps. Looking slyly at the Judge, and then at Kip's worried face, he said heartily, "Well, well, well, Kip. Mighty glad to see you in here."

"Thanks," Kip said gratefully. "Thanks very much."

"I like to see Kip around this building," the Mayor said to the Judge.

"Any particular reason in your case?" the Judge asked dryly.

"Certainly. I'm a great champion of the corrective as opposed to the punitive system. It's men like Kip here who keep a little hope in the hearts of thousands of anti-social characters. I like them to know he's around here." As he put the sheaf of papers on the Judge's desk, he said, "Have a cigar, Kip?"

"Why, thanks," Kip said.

"How about you, Judge?"

"No, thank you."

"All right," he said, breezily. "Come and see me, Kip, and we'll have a talk, eh?" At the door he turned and beamed. "Don't let the Judge lead you astray, Kip. Keep your eye on him," and he puffed out his ruddy cheeks, chuckled to himself and went out.

The Mayor's gestures were all friendly, but they embarrassed Kip. They seemed to be saying, "Another convict — another convict — be friendly to another convict." The Judge couldn't interpret them any other way, and Kip could see he was terribly irritated. His hand sticking out under the hard white cuff on the desk was held tight.

"The Mayor finds you charming, doesn't he?" the Judge said.

"He's a nice guy."

"He's a well-meaning man; you feel bigger than he."

"Geez, no, Judge, no …"

"I could see it in your eyes."

"I took a great liking to him, that's all."

"You like the way he's willing to make a fool of himself over you like thousands of other people in this city. I'm going to talk to you straight," he said, and he got up and walked away and leaned back against the window.

"The Mayor feels so very happy," he said. "He thinks the things he stands for have worked on you," and he smiled. "No man is ever evil in his hierarchy. That's how you get in, Caley. There's no such thing as free will to men like him. Men to him are simply pushed around by forces working on them. They get a man like you in a penitentiary and train him and he expresses the beautiful godhead in him. Everybody is delighted. There's more joy on earth than there is in heaven. Well, I'm having no part of it. You mean well, but I believe that you're potentially dangerous. I have a duty to society — I hope you keep out of trouble — But I'm absolutely opposed to putting you in any position that will glorify you and cheapen my conception of law and order and the people who ought to defend it. That's only sense, isn't it?"

The Judge, tall and straight in the window light, seemed to Kip to have great dignity, and he longed to explain how much he, himself, wanted to be part of the thing the Judge was trying to protect. He ached to tell him he had long ago made peace with himself, and he wanted the Judge to protect his peace for him as he protected the order and peace of the whole city. "You still got me wrong," he said humbly. "You and me can feel the same way – I like the things you say. They hurt a little but they touch something I want."

"Good! Then keep out of trouble," the Judge said, smiling.

"Judge …"

"What?"

"You – you don't really believe I've changed."

"I say I hope you keep out of trouble. Good luck to you."

Kip felt terribly helpless, suddenly. He felt he could never break through that soft, patient voice and touch any yielding warmth. "You're a judge – don't you ever feel you have to give a guy a break even when you don't like him?" he said.

"You make it personal," the Judge said impatiently. "I wish you wouldn't. Look here, justice is like a pattern – the pattern of the common good. It's up to me to see that the pattern isn't broken – just for the sake of fitting you into it. That's exactly why I thought you ought to stay in prison and finish your sentence."

But Kip wasn't listening. He only understood that the Judge thought he ought to be still in prison. He could hear nothing but the beat of marching feet, the scraping of heavy boots, the convict parade, just their legs and their boots swinging by in his head and he got up slowly, pointing his finger at the Judge and whispered, "I know a little guy just like you."

"Really?"

"Yeah. I said I'd see him this afternoon. Whispering Joe used to be the best fur thief in the country. He's just like you. In his own way he says all those things. He's got a great line, too. See, he's good. Maybe you're a damn good judge, too, but the part of you that makes you tick is just the same as the part of Joe. You can't believe in anything. If you didn't you wouldn't be able to sit on that bench day after day and judge everybody.

What have you got that's so big? My guy, Whispering Joe's, got the same thing, whatever it is."

"Good day, Caley."

"All right. I'll go."

"Out – quick," the Judge said. And it was suddenly as it was between them ten years ago when the Judge sentenced him to life and twenty lashes. "My God, Judge, what do you see in me?" he blurted out.

"I said good day."

"Judge, look at me," he said wildly. "Why don't you stay there? Don't back away!"

"I'm not backing away – I'm busy."

"You might as well hate me – you take away my life. Maybe you feel that way about a lot of people. Maybe you sit up there day after day on the bench and know which ones you're going to try and kill off. Yeah, that's it," he whispered. Scared, the Judge backed away. "By the living Jesus," Kip shouted, "didn't you take it out on me? Why weren't you there? Don't you remember? I was a rattlesnake. Well, why didn't you come down? Look, look!" He felt crazy. He mumbled and muttered, wild-eyed, pulling off his coat. "Look, you weren't there. Take a look! It's free." He tossed his coat on the desk, grinning; he jerked his tie off, his shirt, his undershirt, tossing them on the Judge's desk. He wheeled around and thrust his great bare muscular back and shoulders against the Judge's face, almost pinning him to the desk. Strong sunlight from the window shone on the bare back; it shone on the scars that remained from the lashes. The stripes showed a little lighter against the bronzed skin, overlapping, criss-crossing, but mainly circling the back smoothly. "Go on, get an eyeful, twenty lashes! You gave them to me. That's your print on me – your trade mark! Lashed until the blood ran from my body – they're not supposed to draw blood – They gagged me with a halter of gauze to absorb the saliva – I couldn't breathe. If you wanted more why didn't you ask it? Fifteen the first month. The doctors take your pulse – you've got a strong constitution, you're doing fine. 'Keep on going,' he says – six months later I get the rest. I was paying for something. I wanted to get it over. I thought I owed it to people. By God, you'll never be satisfied, will you, Judge?"

But he was out of breath, and the Judge had said nothing. Trembling he reached for his coat. While he was putting it on he rolled up his shirt and stuffed it in his pocket, and he never stopped staring at the Judge.

"How do you like it?" he whispered.

"Caley," the Judge said, quietly. "Take a look at yourself in the mirror over there."

"You look at me!"

"You'll see what I mean. Violence – all violence, a soul full of violence. You're going around with a bomb in your pocket."

"My God, that's all you've been thinking!" Kip whispered, and he backed toward the door.

Seventeen

Holding the turned-up collar of his coat across his neck, he went out to the city hall steps. His back seemed to be burning and he stood on the steps, closing his eyes, and trying to feel where he was. Across the road was the cafeteria, the policeman on a prancing horse, the man closing the bank door, a woman holding a kid over the drinking fountain, and farther down was the blue lake and the rolling bank of sunlit clouds. From the cafeteria came Joe Foley, who had been sitting at the table near the window watching the city hall steps. But Kip didn't see him. He didn't see anything. Everything shone in the sunlight, but he seemed to be walking in darkness. "My God, why did I have to stay there till I acted like he wanted me to? Maybe there's something in me I don't understand. He's sure of it. He felt scared."

Foley was walking beside him. "Heh, how's the repentant one?"

"Eh?"

"How's the light of the world today?"

"Uh."

"You saw the Judge?"

Walking slowly he heard nothing Foley said. Foley, with his long dark hair sticking out under his hat, with his body leaning forward, was grinning at him. "Maybe you've got the Judge lined up now, too, eh? Boy, oh, boy, the Mayor, Maclean, and now the Judge. My God, what a build-up. And all that stuff, every day in the papers. What a man!"

His whispering voice meant nothing to Kip; it was only the Judge's voice, soft, astonished, that he heard. And Foley, sure Kip was listening intently to every word he was saying, grew eager. He said he was glad they could work together again; his dark squinting face shone with triumphant joy. At last Kip seemed willing to listen. Gripping Kip's arm, he whispered, "You just come and go as you please. Who'd ever try to pin anything on you? You can nurse it along a little or take your own time, but Kerrmann and me have got something right in your line …"

"Eh? What's that?" Kip said, the voice just coming in on him.

"The build up you got there."

"What build-up?" Kip said, stopping, puzzled.

"This thing we can work on," Foley said. "Am I talking to myself …"

"Well – why, why …" he said. "Well, for God's sake!" Outraged, he went to swing at Foley; then he controlled himself, but the tip of his finger knocked Foley's glasses off. As he looked down at Foley groping for the glasses, he thought, "See, I didn't hit him. I controlled myself." But he stooped down to help Foley as if Foley belonged to him and anybody could see it.

"I'm sorry, Joe," he said. "I don't know why I did that." He picked up Foley's glasses for him and helped him up. "It was just that I wasn't listening. I was terribly worried about something, and then I woke up and found you thinking I was phony."

"Sure you're a phony," Foley whispered, his hand trembling as he put on his glasses.

"I'll buy you your dinner."

"It's a build-up," Foley shouted, white-faced and wild as Kip pleaded with him. "A build-up, a build-up," he shouted.

"I'll buy you a drink. Come on, kid."

Seeing how sorry and humble Kip was, Foley mumbled, "How am I to know when you're listening? I thought you were agreeing with me. Why didn't you say you weren't?" Then he grinned. "Lend me your car, will you, Kip?" he said suddenly.

"My car?"

"It's what I wanted to see you about."

"What do you want it for?"

"Oh, just to ride around the block," he said, grinning.

Kip dreaded telling Joe he could have the car, for he knew he would take it to mean they had made some kind of a bargain, an admission from him that Foley had this insight into him.

"You can't have the car," he said flatly.

"Why?"

"I'm not taking any chances with stuff like that."

"Why, you big, arrogant bastard," Joe said. "You get a break, you get hold of something that makes you big in this town and then you think you can cut yourself off from the likes of me." His elbows in at his sides, he had pulled away as if he were going to spit at Kip, whispering, half to himself, "Why do you think you're where you are today?"

"It doesn't all come my way, Joe."

"They don't give you the city hall; isn't that tough!"

"Listen ..."

"Who do you think put you up there?" Foley said. "It's guys like me, jailbird. Get that! Guys like me! You climbed on our backs. Who'd be interested in you if it weren't for us? We stick around and be a jailbird back-drop for you, a little fancy window dressing to set you off. But listen, mister! Maybe two or three of us go in for the back to Jesus business, and what does that make you? You've got no patent on your act, you know.

There's only room for one or two like you – you got to have a supporting cast, you got to have a city full of ex-convicts and a jail full of live ones, you big, puffed-up bullfrog. We're featuring you, and you're feeding on us."

"Did I ever high hat you?"

"Just ducking us every day in the week," Foley said, hitting at Kip's loyalty and knowing he couldn't stand it.

"Hell, take the car for the night," Kip said. "All I ask is you just use it yourself, see? If anything goes wrong, I'll beat your ears off."

"Why, thanks, Kip," said Joe, grinning. Kip watched him get in the car and turn on the ignition, his little dark twisted face turned away like a man trying to conceal his satisfaction. The car pulled away and he watched it turn the corner, terribly worried. Foley wanted the car for no good reason. The Judge would have been sure he would lend it to him; Foley was sure too. He walked back to the hotel and into the bar and had a couple of whiskeys, then he sat down by himself in one of the little cubicles. If Foley had planned something and got caught in his car – the Judge would only smile. "I'll kill him – I'll kill him if he gets into trouble in that car," he kept saying. Then he thought, "Whether he does or not he was sure he could wangle it out of me." Putting his head down on his arms he half prayed and then cursed himself. His head felt hot. Everything blurred. He imagined he was out on the street, walking rapidly over to Foley's place above the delicatessen store. The flight of stairs was long and narrow, and he knocked on the door and pushed it open and there was Foley lying on the bed with his shoes off, smoking. A pile of ashes was on the carpet from the burned-out cigarette hanging in his fingers.

"How did you know I'd be in?" Foley said lazily.

"I knew you'd be waiting," he said.

"I'll get my hat," Foley said. He got up and put on his hat and coat. They were out on the street, going along in step. "You had me fooled a minute this afternoon. You didn't think so, but you had me just the same, and I'm hard to fool," Foley said.

Sobbing within himself, Kip looked around wildly. He was still in the bar, only his pulse was racing. At the bar a tall girl in a light fawn coat and a green hat was talking to a little, plump, bulging-eyed blonde with a long bob. Their clothes were shabby, their voices rasped a little. They were two prostitutes, Helen Fisher and Gert Disney, who hung around the hotel and who had had a poor winter. Kip knew them and liked them. He often bought them a drink.

"Sure, he's a big, good-looking guy; that's why they fall for him," Helen, the tall girl, said.

"They say it's a gag."

"Who says it's a gag?"

"You just hear it around."

"Oh, sure, everything's a gag to the wise guys. You're a gag. I'm a gag. I give Kip credit."

"Maybe if I was away a long time I'd get a chance to cool off too."

"They'll never cool you off, Gert. You can take it out in watching him," the tall girl said.

These voices sounded beautiful; the voices of his own people in his own home; there was laughter and loud talk. A few men came in and leaned against the bar; one was big Steinbeck, his face wrinkled up in a big smile.

"Hey, there, fellows," Kip said, getting up. His eyes were bright. He suddenly longed to have them welcome him warmly.

"Hello, Kip – hello, come on and have a drink," they said. "What's stirring?" They wanted him with them; it was lovely.

"You remember me telling you about little Schultz, the guy that loved the corpses," he said, his face full of animation. "I saw him on the street the other day. Where do you think he's working? Why, in an undertaker's parlor, of course. I asked him once why he liked a dead woman better than a live one. What do you think he said? The dead ones stay still!"

"What do you know about that?" they said. They shook their heads and wondered. But Steinbeck was looking at Kip as if there was something strange about him. "Kip, look at you."

"What's the matter?"

"You got no shirt on."

Slowly Kip opened his coat and looked down at his bare breast; then he looked at their startled faces. "Eh, sure, that's funny," he said. He clutched his coat tight across his throat. "There it is in your pocket," somebody said. He pulled the shirt out slowly and looked at it, and then at them as if they were going to say, "Show us your back."

The laughter and good feeling was gone, taken away. He grew frightened. Everything could be taken away quick like that, the things nobody should take. "What a crazy trick," he said. He hurried up to his room and put his shirt on feverishly. Then he went out to the street in the fine March twilight with the spring smell in the air, going along with his big strides. All the sights and sounds seemed more and more to belong to the dream he had had till tonight, to Julie and the brightness between them. When he got to the school yard, the fountain rippling in the night air had a lonely sound, and when he was going up the stairs and the old janitor bowed to him, he didn't notice him.

He didn't knock on Julie's door, he pushed it open and strode in and stood in the middle of the room, waiting. Julie came running out of the bathroom, scared. She was wearing a blue dressing gown. "Kip, it's you – I wondered who it was," she said.

"It's me."

"What's the matter?"

"Nothing."

"You've no tie on."

"I forgot it," he said. "What's the difference?"

Maybe looking at him, she felt what had happened because she wanted to speak and couldn't; she suddenly looked desolate. "I waited for you to phone me last night," she said.

"There was nothing to say."

"Nothing?"

When she shook her head like that, heartbroken, it only mattered that nothing should be lost; he had to do something to make her a part of him. "Julie, come here," he said, and she came to him, frightened at what she knew had happened, putting her arms up around his neck. "Harder, like this," he said. Then he was jerking her dressing gown off roughly.

"Please, don't," she begged him.

He didn't see the pain in her eyes. He only knew that the thing he wanted to feel no one in the world could take from him was in her. She suddenly started pounding his head with her fists. He was terribly surprised. "I guess I knew you'd do that," he whispered. "By God, I knew it."

Backing away, she swung a chair in front of her. "Don't, Kip, don't," she pleaded with him. "Not like this. This isn't the way we've felt. Look at your face. You look crazy."

"Stand there and keep talking to me. Sure – I'm all right to talk to."

"Don't feel like that about me, Kip," she whispered.

He was edging around the chair slowly, mumbling, "Sure, I'm all right to sit around with. But I'm not one of your cloak and suit friends. When it comes to this, when I get down to brass tacks with you, I'm out. I scare you." Then he shouted. "That's right, stare at me. Take a look." And he laughed crazily. "I just wanted you to tell it to me in your own way when I turned on the pressure."

She came from behind the chair, her face full of gentleness. "Kip, what did the Senator say?"

"To hell with that. Come here," he said. "You're stalling."

She let him grab her and pick her up in his arms. When she

lay against him, not struggling, but with her eyes soft and her mouth opened a little, everything seemed to break.

"Coming along the street I knew it was going to be like this," he said. "I knew if I tried to take you you'd push me away. Only I kept thinking it couldn't be." He was staring down at her, whispering almost to himself. "Things come close to me, then they pull away. The things I want most."

But her eyes were closed and she seemed to be broken. It weakened him. He let her sit down on the couch and sat apart from her, his head in his hands, trying to push off a sudden overwhelming loneliness.

"You didn't hurt me, Kip," she said, putting her hand on his shoulder.

"I got to destroy things, I guess."

"It wasn't that I didn't want you," she said, coming close to him. "But everything between us has been so fine – I wanted it to come when we were both feeling gentle."

"And I spoiled it."

"Oh, Kip," she said. "Hold me, hold me terribly tight – I do want you." Her eyes were soft and warm. When he pulled her dressing gown off and looked at her small breasts, and the mole on her shoulder, he said huskily, "It's terribly beautiful."

Smiling up at him, she held him tighter against her; he tried hard to fold her into him forever, forgetting everything.

He was lying beside her and she asked him to turn out the light. "I'm glad," she said. "It's all right, Kip." It made him think suddenly of walking in the snow with her when she told him about her childhood and the things she had wanted.

"You're just a kid," he said.

"Why don't you talk to me and tell me about it?"

His big hand was gripping her arm terribly tight. He told her about the Senator; then he said, "I guess the Judge made me feel I might always be on the outside looking in." When he stopped, faltering, he was really thinking, "I didn't hit Foley; I controlled myself." As he held her arm tight, he felt the beginning of a feeling of security. If he had just been violent, he couldn't have that feeling. In reaching out desperately for her he had been only trying to make sure of her warmth and faith, more necessary to him than any ambitions.

"The Judge doesn't understand it," she said. "He thinks all that people want is to be protected from things. That's crazy – you can't live on his law and order – everybody wants something that breaks it and makes their hearts feel free."

She seemed to be far closer to people than the Judge could ever be. She said the things he wanted to think. His enormous faith in himself began to rise again. Noises from the street, the voices of passing people, reminded him of what he meant to so many like them who wouldn't understand anything the Judge had said, any more than the Judge understood what they really wanted. "I should do the work I want to do anyway," he said. "How can he stop me?"

Eighteen

H E BEGAN to do the kind of work he had planned to do on the parole board. He went out among old convicts he knew around the city. He talked to their wives. If they were hard up and discouraged he loaned them money. When he met a young jailbird who was bitter about being trailed by police he felt happy if he could persuade him to go to the city hall with him for a frank discussion with a police inspector whom he would ask to take his word for it that this jailbird was on the level. He was friendly with old habitual criminals too, as long as he didn't hear of one of them urging some heartbroken kid to commit a crime again. The old ones who had known him in prison liked him and were a little afraid of him. At nights he sat around in the restaurant talking to people. He seemed to be very busy; jailbirds were coming in all the time asking for him. Then the police began to come too. He was certainly useful to them. An inspector often used to sit down and talk with him for an hour. In watching him they could watch most of the old crooks in town. For a while Jenkins didn't notice this stream of crooks and jailbirds to the hotel. The racing season had come on and the place was crowded with jockeys and trainers and track troupers from far-away places. There was a lot of easy money around; all the little tarts in town were hanging around the hotel. Kip and Julie themselves were at the track every afternoon. But when the track crowd moved on, the hotel seemed to be empty. There was a lot of time for Kip to sit listening to the troubles and temptations of old crooks, pitying them and trying to help them.

"I don't like the way things are shaping up around here," Jenkins said to him. "Am I supposed to like this collection of mugs sitting around the dining room watching everybody that pulls out a dollar bill? They're all dead beats themselves."

"You got it wrong," Kip said. "Things are a little slow around here because of the hot weather coming on."

"You shouldn't have time for that cross-eyed tribe."

"If a woman comes around here for a little advice, shouldn't I give it to her? If the police send some poor guy to have a talk with me, should I see him?"

"Look, Kip, this place ain't exactly a hospital."

"Whoever said it was?"

"Nor a domestic relations court."

"It's a hotel."

"Sure and not a school of sociology," Jenkins said. But Kip figured Jenkins was quarrelsome because one of the boys he had used in the white hope tournament had got killed and the newspapers were insisting he pay for the funeral.

One night a scared little man with a drooping black moustache and a coat far too big for him pounded on Kip's door. His coat was torn. He was pleading desperately with his eyes, without even opening his mouth. The police were chasing him, he said. He had stolen a diamond ring from a jewelry store window. His wrist was badly cut and there was blood on the sleeve of his coat.

"I got four kids," he said. "I got a wife and four kids and they got no clothes. Please, Mr. Caley, I've never been in trouble. I worked in a tailor's shop twenty years. I lose two fingers in the wife's washing machine. I'm out of work, years. Please, Mr. Caley, let me stay here. No one'll ever think of looking in your place for me."

Everything that had happened in his life seemed to be laid out there in the lines of his twitching face. Kip understood why the tailor had turned to him, of all people in the city, and he was very moved. Telling him to lie down and stay there the night, he took his coat to the bathroom and washed the blood from the sleeve. But while he listened to the little man sucking in breath, almost hearing the pumping of his heart, he began to be bothered. He felt disloyal to everybody. Was he joining himself to this little tailor against them, he asked himself. Yet the loyalty to the wretched tailor seemed to come out of the deepest part of his being. When he went downstairs to the restaurant he felt miserable. He made up his mind to go and see Father Butler and ask him if he was betraying the people who trusted him. The next day he made the trip with Julie. On the drive across the country to Littletown near the penitentiary where Father Butler had his parish house, she kept telling him fervently she would have done what he had done. It was beautiful driving with her through the rolling country, watching the sun glistening on the flat surfaces of rocks sticking out of bare fields. Whenever they were on a high hill they stopped the car and watched the fields roll away to the blue sky.

The priest was overjoyed to see them, for few visitors ever came to his house. They had a dinner that was a banquet. Afterwards, in the dark, they sat on the front porch and rocked back and forth and the boards squeaked. The sound of crickets came from along the dark country road, a nighthawk was screeching around the house, and beyond the town were the hills and the prison.

"How's the Senator?" the priest asked.

"I don't see much of him. Of course, I've been pretty busy," he said. His voice sounded loud in the night air, but it broke a little, talking about his work.

The priest was troubled. It was splendid work, he said, but Kip must be very careful that he didn't give all of himself to the underworld. The men in the prison still spoke of him; they liked to hear about him because he still gave them hope for themselves. Kip told how he had hidden the tailor. He made it very clear that he dreaded violating the trust people had in him, yet he wanted to show he believed the sympathy he had for the tailor was part of the same great sympathy people had had for him. There was in the world a great well of charity; people had drawn on it for him; he felt he had only drawn on it again for the little tailor. He tried to see the priest's face in the dark. When he heard him sucking at his pipe, he knew by the silence he wasn't condemned. "What would you have done?" he kept asking Father Butler.

"Maybe the same thing," he replied slowly. "I don't know, I really couldn't say. I wouldn't say I wouldn't do it." And Kip understood that a man could violate the law in such a way his goodness would not be broken, but would be strengthened; charity came before law and order. It seemed to give him even more freedom.

When they were going, and the priest and Kip were standing down at the car waiting for Julie to come from the house, the priest said, "Ah, she's a lovely personality. What does she do, Kip?"

"She's a gambler."

"Oh, be serious. She's just a child."

"She's a model."

"You stir her up, you fill her with eagerness – you keep everything bright for her. Look at her coming! She's lovely. She's good for you. I'll be in the city all next week, why don't you both come and see me?" he said.

Driving along the road in the dark with the headlights shining on the curved leaves of the willows, Kip asked her, "How do you like him?"

"He's a peach."

"You know what?"

"No, what?"

"You ought to marry me. Let him marry us when he comes to the city next week."

"Such a strange thing to say to a girl."

"I'd like to have about six kids."

"If I'm just a kid – that would make seven."

"All right – lucky seven."

They drove along in the dark and when they came to a bridge over a narrow ravine they stopped the car to listen to the sound of running water. She wanted to go down and sit by the stream. They climbed over the old fence and half slid down the bank, and there was a flat field of pastureland between the banked-up road and the trees along the stream, and there was thick dew on the long grass. Their feet swished through the grass. Picking her up in his arms, he carried her across the field in the moonlight. Suddenly he stopped and looked all around, listening to the stream and the rustling noises, and feeling her lying against him.

"What's the matter?" she said.

"It just seems so funny being here."

"What's funny about it?"

"It's not a thing I would ever have thought of doing."

"Put me down."

"No."

"Then go on."

As he walked on he said softly, "It's hard to figure out the way things shape themselves. I start off heading for somewhere, and then I'm here, and it seems farther off than I ever thought of going. It's kind of hard to figure."

"It's a mystery," she said.

"But that doesn't tell you anything. A girl like you could be in a lot of other places."

"No, it's the red pavilion."

"What?"

"That's a poem," she said. "Leave thy father and thy mother

and thy brother, who hath the red pavilion of my heart." They were going down the slope, and he had to put her down, and they went on down pushing branches aside. It was hard to get close to the edge of the stream. They followed it down to a little pond in a clearing that shone bright in the moonlight. Old logs, jammed together, had made a little dam. They sat down on a patch of grass on the bank and Julie took off her shoes and stockings and let her feet hang in the cool water, and he sat beside her, listening to the night noises. When he was drying her feet with his handkerchief, letting the little cold foot rest in the palm of his big hand, he began to feel the most puzzling kind of new freedom.

Nineteen

THEY DIDN'T get back to the city till half-past three in the morning. Kip didn't wake up till the middle of the afternoon. When he was dressing, Jenkins came in. Kip thought he was going to complain about him being away yesterday. But Jenkins was surprisingly friendly.

"That's a nice pair of shoulders you got, Kip," he said, watching him dressing. "Ever do any wrestling?"

"It's a thing I don't take to," Kip said.

"I'm on my way down to the Three Star Club. Why don't you come along and have a workout with Steinbeck?"

"What for?"

"I'd like to see how you go," Jenkins said. "My God, look at those shoulders. Stand beside me! Look! I'm just up to your shoulder." As Jenkins lost weight the true lines of his face and his eyes began to emerge from the puffy flesh. The eyes seemed colder. "Pick me up, Kip," Jenkins said. "Go on, pick me up." Kip suddenly grabbed him around the huge soft belly, hoisting him high, spinning around, pivoting on his heels and going faster; then he let him go and dropped him like a great bag of sand on the carpet, where he lay white-faced and dizzy.

"You said pick you up, didn't you? Here's where I pick you

up," he said. Laughing, he picked him up and helped him over to the couch.

Holding his dizzy head, Jenkins said, "It's all right, it's all right, I asked for it. My God, and I still weigh two hundred and eighty-seven pounds." When his head cleared his face began to shine with happiness. "You'd be a wonder. I can see you in tights. I'd love Steinbeck to see you."

"Steinbeck's seen me," Kip said.

"You should keep in shape. You're letting your blood get sluggish, sitting around. What do you say?" Kip was glad of a chance to create a better feeling between them.

"Maybe I've been letting myself get soft," he said. "Let's go."

They drove down to the Three Star Club next door to a burlesque show, and climbed a long, badly lighted flight of stairs, with a trail of cigarette butts all the way up. At the top Jenkins rapped six times, three short and three long. "The boys run a little book in here and take a few bets so you don't just walk in," he said. A little Jew with a big cigar let them into a room with a ring in the center. Steinbeck and a young heavyweight wrestler were working out in the ring. A few men, all with their hats on, were sitting around watching the wrestlers.

Kip and Jenkins watched old Steinbeck mechanically repeating a strange hold on the young heavyweight. Steinbeck, a great black mat of hair on his chest, grimacing horribly, slugged the kid on the jaw with his elbow, dragged him over to the ropes, hoisted up the lower rope with this free hand, forced down the middle rope with his knee, jerked the head in and then let the ropes snap out straight on the neck. The green boy tried to kick his legs and roll his eyes and choke like a strangled man. And Kip began to laugh. The dull, young face showed no suffering. Disgusted, Jenkins yelled, "Oh, cut it out, cut it out. That lug's got no emotion and no talent."

"It's a lousy act, eh?" Kip asked.

"Not even an act with that mug. How the hell is Steinbeck going to strangle a guy on the ropes if the guy won't look strangled? Go get yourself a pair of tights and have some fun. I'll talk to Steinbeck."

Kip looked a foot taller than old Steinbeck, and so big, wild-eyed and dark, the gentlemen on the chairs around the wall got up and stood around the ring. "Just take it easy, Kip," Steinbeck said, in the soft, patient voice. "Let's see if you've got a natural sense of leverage, see how you use your strength. Grab hold of me. Try and throw me." Kip grinned and jumped at him and knocked him over with his weight. Their bodies scraped on the resin; they bounced and rolled and heaved; his muscles tightened; it became like a joy that had long been denied him. The smell of the sweat was good, too, and the strain with all his heart and guts as he tried to roll squat Steinbeck, using no grip, just heaving with his natural strength, beautifully forgetting everything. But there was no yielding in Steinbeck's shoulders, just a deceptive rolling away. And then came sudden desperate unbelief, a tightening, a sobbing for breath as his arms grew lifeless the way Steinbeck held them. And Steinbeck was calling to Jenkins, "I guess I'd have to break it, mister, to roll him."

Steinbeck's calm voice suddenly broke through his violence, like the Judge had broken through it, telling him to look in the mirror.

"Steinie. I wasn't going to hurt you, was I? You didn't think I was, did you, Steinie?" he gasped.

"Old Steinie doesn't get hurt, son," he said. He slapped Kip affectionately on the head and got up and strolled amiably over to the ropes, looking like a thoughtful mechanic who had just tried out the engine of an old car. Kip was ashamed of his violence. Going off by himself to the shower, he heard Jenkins asking eagerly, "How do you figure him?"

He got under the shower and cooled down and was thinking he could apologize to Steinbeck, when Jenkins came in and yelled so he could be heard above the spluttering water, "Steinie thinks you're bad-tempered, Kip."

"I'll apologize."

"He's kidding – But I think I got a new angle on you."

"On me?"

"Look at it in this way," Jenkins said. "There's a lot of people in this town that'd like to have a chance to see you and they just naturally never get down to the hotel. I figure old Steinbeck could take you in hand and teach you enough to get by on and we keep you dark for maybe the first twelve bouts. You win them all, see? I'll give you that in black and white – a contract you win your twelve bouts, and then everybody gets excited, wondering who you are. I like that part. Then we throw you in against somebody near the top, see? We get the newspapers to cooperate and give you a grand build-up. Then, pop, it's out of the bag. You're Kip Caley. It's a sensation!"

Kip only looked at him blankly. He came out of the shower, standing naked beside Jenkins, his big body glowing red and the water streaming off him. "You nearly fooled me. You're kidding, aren't you?" he said, and tried to laugh.

"Like hell I am."

"But – don't you see what it would make me?"

"What?"

"It's all crooked – I'd be a phony."

"Aw, don't be so coy."

"What do you think people would say?"

"I don't know what they'd say, but I've a damn good idea we'd get a couple of good gates out of it. What do you say?"

It had come at him very quickly and he wasn't ready; he only knew everything he stood for was being challenged.

Grabbing a towel, he started rubbing his head. "Are you going to play ball or not?" Jenkins asked.

"Why, no – of course I'm not," he said simply.

"Come on, take off the high hat," Jenkins said, looking pretty sullen.

"Listen, I couldn't do that, not me. You must be crazy."

"Maybe I'm crazy," Jenkins said. "But if you won't string along with me you're through at the hotel; that's all I got to say. Take a couple of hours to think it over." Looking pretty sore, he waddled out.

Kip rubbed his body with the towel. He held his clothes, fumbling with them, and couldn't believe he was there and it had happened. He forgot to comb his wet hair. He went out leaving his hat there.

Outside, with the crowd from the burlesque show streaming past and the red sun shining like a great fireball rolled to the end of the street, he was suddenly astonished that he hadn't punched Jenkins on the nose. Bareheaded, his wet hair matted on his forehead, he stood there. People bumped into him and he felt apologetic to them all. "If I popped him I'd lose the job right then, see?" As if the job was just as important to them all as it was to him, because they all had faith in him – enormous faith. And jailbirds, paroled men, boys trying to go straight – suppose they came to the hotel and found he wasn't there? "But if I keep the job and turn phony?" A little guy in a straw hat and gray flannels brushed past him. He wanted to grab him and say, "Look, I'm Kip Caley. If you heard I was a phony – never mind what kind – but a phony, well ..." Backing up against the lamp-post the little guy would take off his hat and wipe his head and look terribly hurt.

"Jesus, you're the one guy I'd have sworn was on the level," he would gasp. "What in hell in this town is on the level then?" Walking along with his big slow stride, Kip thought: "Jenkins's given me no choice. What'll I do?"

As he wandered along the streets, the sound of his own footfalls seemed to worry him all the more, and he wanted to sit down somewhere and try and solve his problem. He found himself climbing the stairs to the Ping Pong pool parlor, an old hangout he hadn't been in for years. No one saw him come in. He sat down on the bench by the wall and watched the pyramids of light over the green tables shining on hands and arms and colored balls moving under them. Crossing his knees, he put his chin in his hands and sat there worrying.

Then someone called from the second table, "Why, look what the wind blew in," and he looked up in wonder. It was Foley in his shirt sleeves, playing pool with Kerrmann, who had a fine, expensive suit on. They came over, grinning, carrying their cues. Open-mouthed, he watched them. Hardly believing he had wandered in there, the last place in the world to find anyone to help him with his problem. "Heh, gang, here's the friend of the people," Foley called. Laughing boys came gliding to him out of the shadows, carrying their billiard cues.

"My goodness, he ain't got his white tie and tails on," Kerrmann said.

"Can't a guy do a little slumming?" Foley said.

"He should bring his big friends with him."

"Just a minute," Foley said, his voice growing eager. Bending down he squinted at Kip's worried face. "Look at him!" he said excitedly. "What's bothering him? Are they treating their boy right, Kip?"

They put him apart from them like this. They mocked him, but suddenly his face brightened. They knew he had big friends. They made him think of Senator Maclean. "I was just passing the time. I'm on my way now," he said, and he grinned at them. It was magical; it had happened in this place; the knot tightening in him was suddenly loosened. Jenkins wouldn't listen to him; but he would have to listen to Senator Maclean who had two mortgages on his hotel. And he hurried down the stairs.

Twenty

THE CARILLON bell was ringing and groups of girls from the graduation party were floating across the grass in the twilight when he passed the university campus on the way to the Senator's place. Everything he saw seemed to quicken his hope in the Senator. When the maid let him in he saw Ellen coming along the hall, dressed to go out.

"Hello, Ellen," he said eagerly.

"Oh, hello," she said. Her face was cool and sullen, as it had been the first night he had seen her.

"I wanted to see your father – but how have you been?" He wanted her to be glad, her eyes to shine. But she hardly turned on her way out.

"Fine, thanks," she said. "I don't know whether Father should see anybody. He's been in bed." And she said to the maid, "Will you see, Hilda?" And drawing on her gloves, with her cool little smile, she said, "Excuse me." She went out as if he had never touched her.

It upset him. Then he thought she was probably embarrassed, remembering she had lain in his arms. But the maid was leading him up to the Senator's bedroom. And soon he heard the Senator saying to someone, "I'll see him, I'll see him."

The Senator was lying on the bed in his blue silk pyjamas,

and a maid was massaging the muscles of his legs. His white hair was mussed all over his head. His face looked bloated, but the back of his neck was as rosy as ever. He had been drinking heavily for two days. Kip was terribly disappointed to see the Senator in this condition. "What are you staring at me for?" the Senator said irritably. "Why don't you sit down?"

"It's just a little thing I wanted," Kip said.

"You want something, too. Everybody wants something."

"This is just a simple thing you can do in two minutes," Kip said, and he got up and went close to the Senator. He wanted to break through the Senator's bad humor and make him feel how important they had been to each other. He went close to the bed. "We haven't been in touch with each other much and maybe you don't know how it's going for me. I'm going to lose my job – I had a run-in with Jenkins today," he said.

"There's no distinction in that," the Senator said. His voice was muffled because his head was buried in the pillow. "Everybody has a run-in with Jenkins. If that's all you've got to worry you, you're pretty lucky." Then he groaned. "My legs twitch – I can't feel anything." The maid stopped massaging a moment, her hands poised delicately. "I took a terrible trimming last week," the Senator went on. "I figure it cost me about a million dollars. That damn Golden Bear mine! I floated that company, see? We sell a million shares of stock and we drill and don't hit anything and I advise abandoning the whole thing. The shareholders jump down my throat and sue me. The shares go down to a nickel ..." But Kip was looking so unhappy, the Senator said, "Ada, go and get him a drink. He's not listening."

"I don't want a drink," Kip said. "I was listening."

But the girl went out and the Senator sat up in bed and flung his arms wide. "And what does Crighton do? He sneaks up there with an engineer and drills and hits it. He buys up most of the stock at a nickel a share. It jumps to four dollars a share. I'm frozen out!"

"I guess you feel pretty terrible, Senator," Kip said. "But here's something that'll give you a laugh. I'm going to lose my job because Jenkins wants to turn me into a wrestler."

"Well – well – well – leave it to Jenkins to think of something like that," the Senator said. "He'd promote his grandmother."

"That's it," Kip said more eagerly. "He wants to make a phony out of me – give me a contract guaranteeing I win so many matches. Just another phony! It doesn't enter his head people would feel hurt, people that come to the hotel and feel they did a grand thing helping me, see?" His face was bright with faith in all the people who had come to see him.

"If there's another cent to be squeezed out of anything, Jenkins'll certainly go after it," the Senator said.

"That's right."

"What do you want me to do?"

"He'll do what you say."

The Senator swung his legs wearily over the side of the bed. He rubbed his white hair and sighed. He stared at Kip with his bloodshot eyes. He looked as if someone had just hung a millstone around his neck. "Look, Kip, if you're fed up with Jenkins, why don't you go up to the mining country. The whole future of this country is the mines – that's where all the big opportunities are going to be."

"Go away?" he said astonished.

"Sure."

"Leave everything?"

"I have to go places I don't want to go," the Senator said. "I lie awake at night thinking of the summer salmon run and the woods, but can I go fishing?" He looked up suddenly like a thwarted child. "Can I?"

"This job is terribly important to me."

"It is?"

"Yes."

"Then string along with Jenkins. If he thinks there's money

in you wrestling, there probably is, but try and get a check in advance, see? That's a tip."

"It wouldn't be on the level."

"Now, Kip," the Senator said mildly as he looked up at Kip's big impatient dark face, "any newspaperman'll tell you it's the way they do things – you've got to allow for a little leeway."

"He doesn't get it," Kip said. It seemed incredible. He was staring at this man who had come to him in the prison to tell him how people felt about him, how they wanted him out, how truly they believed in him. This man with the white, wondering, sick face had given him his life. He had opened up the big world of important people to him. Now he felt he had never known the Senator. How could he have known him if he never knew the things that were really important to him?

"What don't I get?" the Senator asked, surprised.

"The dirty thing this is," he wanted to shout at him. "I've got to explain it to you," he said. He looked terribly surprised. "This is funny – I used to listen to you," his voice grew soft with wonder. "You said some swell things, coming to me in prison. I remember – it's funny me being here trying to help you see this. You're a funny guy."

"Me!" the Senator said indignantly. "I help you and get you one job and something happens and I try to tell you to try your luck in mining country. What is this? What's happened to you?"

"You did a big generous thing," Kip said softly. "You spoke for millions of people – they wanted you to. But you don't seem to understand what you did, or what you said for them."

"What do you mean?" the Senator said. He got up slowly in his bare feet, and shook his head anxiously, as if he had just been told that nothing in his life had any true moral value.

"I mean you don't get the significance of the thing," Kip whispered. "My God, you and me – we built up something big and beautiful for people. And you forget what it was like – you forget!" He was muttering to himself. "It came right here into his own house – all those big people – and New Year's Eve – how moved they were, the way they sang." His face shone. He seemed to be hearing people crying out to him and feeling their wonder as they thronged around him. "Okay, Senator, I'm on my way," he said. And he started to go.

"Wait – you can't say that to me. I helped you," the Senator said. His step faltering, his hand out, he came after Kip. He looked terribly humiliated. "I'd go up to the mines myself if I were younger. That's where things happen quickly. You might get rich," he said. Then he stopped; the muscles of his legs twitched and failed him. His knees sagged. He put his hand down on the floor.

Looking back, Kip pitied him. He felt maybe he had always been a bigger man than the Senator. "So long," he said. "I guess you dropped out somewhere along the way."

Twenty-One

WHEN HE got out in the summer night air he stopped a minute by the lamp-post. The air was sultry; there was no breeze. He broke into a sweat. Wiping his head with his handkerchief, he thought desperately, "The Senator's lost sight of it, that's all; he didn't measure up to his own big talk." But the rumble and hum of the city traffic seemed to carry all the warmth and faith of city people to him. All his confidence in his own power was stirred. He wanted to show Jenkins how important he was to the hotel customers. "If Jenkins tries to club me into going his way, I'll pull out – but not before everybody knows about it."

He longed to be among people and feel he touched them magically. He wanted to offer them his loyalty, too. He hurried back to the hotel and went straight to Jenkins' office. Jenkins wasn't there. Wandering around the lobby, he smiled at everybody; he went into the bar and shook hands warmly with Eddie. A lazy, dream-like smile was on his face; he bowed to people coming in. Then he went over to Billie at the desk and said, "Tell Jenkins when he comes in, I'm waiting in the tavern."

At the table near the big palm, Jones, the bald-headed credit clothier, who had a big sign out at the ball park offering a suit of clothes to the ball player who hit it with a home run, was sitting with Treacy, the secretary of the ball club, and a girl in a black dress and red shoes.

"This guy Molsen hits my sign twice this afternoon," Jones was moaning. "It cost me two suits of clothes and there weren't two hundred people in the grandstand. What do I get out of it?"

"How many suits do you figure it cost you all year?" the secretary said.

"Eighteen. Do you want me to go bankrupt? Why don't you get some pitchers and stop those guys?"

Their conversation seemed to be about such trivial, homely little things, Kip wanted to quicken everything for them. Bowing to the lady, he sat down. "It's funny how you remember the feel of a night. Coming into the hotel …" he began.

"Yeah – hello, Kip," the clothier said. "Like I say, if you had taken Leake out in the seventh when they started hitting him –" he went on.

Kip looked puzzled; but he was sure they couldn't have heard him. "I mean the way it feels like rain out on the street, heavy and sultry," he said dreamily, smiling at them.

"It wasn't hot at the game. There was a cool breeze," the girl said.

"It's nights like these when a guy's broke that gets him into trouble," he said, a little more emphatically.

The secretary shrugged, "Who said anything about being broke?" he asked. They all looked at Kip with dead faces; they looked at each other and raised their eyebrows.

"As I say, imagine letting a guy like Leake stay in the box and blow a four run lead –" the clothier went on. But Kip leaned closer to them, touched suddenly by that quick panic he had felt coming out of the Senator's house; it seemed to rise in him; he crushed it out of him with all his eagerness.

Leaning away then, looking from one to the other, he said, "What I meant was it was a night like this when we planned that big mail robbery – you remember, don't you, twelve years ago?" There was no chance of stopping him now. But they didn't seem to remember; he grew uncertain. "Why, it was the biggest thing in the country at the time." When they still looked impatient, he went on desperately. "They said it might have been planned by a great captain, you remember? Some guy said it was done with the skill of Hannibal planning to cross the Alps. Well, that's right, you don't remember: the money was in this armored car and there didn't seem to be anything on the street but a peddler with a pushcart, a coal wagon and an Italian with a hurdy-gurdy." His face was flushed. A strange eagerness was creeping into his voice. The girl took out her mirror and started rubbing her chin, as if she had heard the story before. "Give us a pencil," he said.

He began to sketch on the tablecloth. "There was only one outlet to the highway, see?" he said. "See, here it is – right here. There's no use rushing bull-headed into these things. Now – watch – the guards start having a little chat. Angelo, with the pushcart, pulls out the machine gun and Angelo at the hurdy-gurdy lets fly from the other side, shooting high. I'm there on the coal truck, seeing everything's going fine as silk."

"How much did you get?" Jones asked indifferently. "That's the point."

"One hundred and fifty thousand," he said easily.

"Holy Moses, did you hear that?" Jones said.

On their faces was that look of childish wonder. It seemed very beautiful to him. It had taken a long time to come, but it was there. He smiled happily, with immense relief.

"That's a hell of a lot of money," they kept saying. "An awful lot of money. Boy, oh, boy, one hundred and fifty grand in one shot!"

"If you're just thinking of the money," he said, carelessly toying with them in his exultation, "how much do you figure I've taken in banks all told?"

"How much?"

"At least six hundred thousand dollars, maybe more."

They all looked amazed. "Why, gee, Kip, what did you do with it?"

"Six hundred thousand dollars! Did you hear that, Steve?"

"Why don't you make yourself a little money and get in the big league like Kip here?" the girl said. "Have you still got any of it, Kip?" she whispered.

But he saw Billie the Butcher Boy gliding over to the table. "I told Jenkins, Kip – He's waiting," Billie said.

Stirred by the unbelieving wonder in their faces, Kip got up and left them. He knew they were following him with rapt expressions. His fine big feeling was at its peak, when he went into Jenkins' office.

Jenkins was sitting at the desk with the wide tips of his fingers held together in an arch, the light tapering up from the pyramid base of his three great chins to his forehead. Rolling up to the desk with his big stride, his eyes a little wild, Kip said, "I was in here earlier looking for you."

"All steamed up, eh?" Jenkins said sourly.

"You bet I am."

"That sounds good for both of us," Jenkins said. "Maybe I can blow the whistle right now."

"Wait a minute," Kip said, leaning over the desk. "You know I like this job. You understand that – it works in with a lot of plans I have – I'd like to keep it. I don't feel cheap saying it, you understand? But get this, Mister Jenkins: if you think the job is bigger than me, bigger than the things I've wanted –" Straightening up he held his arms out wide. "Why, you're simply crazy," he said.

"Too big for the job, eh?" Jenkins gasped. "My, God, this is funny."

"It's not funny, no, sir. You and your job aren't going to spoil my life," he said.

"You say that to me?"

"Sure."

"I spoil your cockeyed life?"

"Trying to hit me over the head with the job if I won't turn phony for you."

"So I have to sit here listening to more of that stuff?" Jenkins said. He got wild himself. He slapped his fat palms on the desk. "You stand there like a Y.M.C.A. secretary – it gripes me, Caley, it gripes me – I want to make you a crook! There's gratitude! Gratitude in a big dose of purity league horseshit. A pretty lofty guy for a jailbird, eh?" He was outraged.

But Kip only smiled at him. "Trying to get me sore, eh?" he said. "Maybe you want me to bat you down and then you'll get me pinched, eh?"

Then Jenkins seemed to be truly puzzled. "Maybe I'm crazy – but do you really think I'm firing you because I want to make some money out of you on a proposition you think is crooked?"

"Certainly."

"Well, for Christ's sake," he said, astonished. "You're wonderful! Have you been blind around here, or do you only come in from romping in the country to have tea now and again? Where are all those fine friends of yours? Instead of a crowd with some money, what do we get? A lot of jailbirds and their wives, your pals, hanging around getting cross-eyed every time anybody pulls out a bill."

"You cheapen everybody who ever came around here to get a little help," Kip said. He spanned the length of the desk with his great arms. Then he started to laugh excitedly, liking the struggle. His laughter seemed to be winding him up, poising his big outraged wildness before he let it go.

"Don't get rough around here, Caley," Jenkins said.

"I've a mind to, Mister Jenkins."

"I'll get big Steinbeck to throw you out the window. He can do it too, don't forget."

"You insult me, you insult thousands of other people."

"Wait a minute," Jenkins shouted. He looked incredulous,

as if the dream in Kip, the exaltation, the way he saw himself, the thing he thought he was, was just touching him for the first time. He wanted to get a good wondering look at him. "You must be a little screwy," he said. "I didn't get it – I don't quite get it now – But how should I know? I was just trying to tell you it was money made the world go round. I guess I been missing you by a mile. I didn't know you had jumped the tracks. What is this big thing you think you are?"

"You wouldn't understand."

"I want to understand – what do you think you've been doing around here for months?"

"Letting people see what a little good will can do for a man."

"Letting the cops use you to keep track of all the crooks in town, you mean."

"Use me?"

"And letting crooks use this place as a clubhouse."

"Go ahead, cheapen everything."

"I didn't start this. It was you that had the gall to say I was trying to remind people what you are."

"You wanted to do it in your own rotten way."

"Hasn't that been your job around here, letting them know who you are, or am I stupid?"

"Look how you put it!"

"And they don't come any more."

"Well …"

"They don't."

"So I should shout, 'Look out everybody, I'm a bank robber. Whoooooo!'"

Jenkins was completely disgusted; his puffing red face seemed to be bloated with indignation.

"What the hell have you been shouting for months that used to entertain them – your Y.M.C.A. record?"

"What?"

"This afternoon I was trying to give you a hand up – trying

to make you a drawing-card again – they're tired of you around here, that's all."

"That's a terrible lie," Kip said. But he was leaning on the desk limply, struggling with his own surprise. He looked stricken. It made him think of the Senator telling him to go away, wanting to get rid of him, of Ellen, with no time to talk. He kept staring helplessly at Jenkins. He couldn't speak. Then he felt new, fresh and frightening surprise. He must have known what people wanted to talk about. Hadn't he practically cried out to the clothier and his friends, "Look at me – for Christ's sake, look at me – can't you see I'm the biggest bandit that ever walked in these parts?" as if he knew it was the only reason he was important to people– There seemed to be a little tug at his heart, a sudden distortion of his vision. Everything he had thought good became ugly and ridiculous. His big hands tightened on the desk. The bones whitened in the light. Jenkins began to look scared again.

"Maybe the Judge was right," Kip whispered.

"The Judge? What's that?"

"You don't need to look scared, Jenkins," he said softly. "I'm clowning – I was clowning in there talking to Jonesy – I've been clowning for months."

But he looked so wild, desolate and broken, Jenkins called nervously, "Heh, Kip, where are you going?"

"Just on my way," he said, going out to the lobby.

Leaning on the desk he grinned into people's faces. But he felt lost – pushed out of his place, mumbling, as if he was saying to everybody, "I was right there, mister – that was my place. I paid for it. I mean I think that was the place. You're trying to get me mixed up – look – don't you remember me? Look at the number on my ticket ... that's funny – I can't find the ticket ... Say, maybe I'm wrong – what's the name of this place?"

He went into the bar, his face like a mask. Eddie was

shaking up a Tom Collins for a lady drinker at the other end of the bar. "I'm on my way, Eddie," he said, watching his face.

"Is this something new?"

"I just heard it."

"I sort of saw it coming," Eddie said sympathetically. He had a good and generous heart. "I hope you're not on your uppers, Kip," he said. "I hope you took it while it was coming. Have a drink on me?"

"Something large and cool. My head feels hot," he said.

He had two drinks and then he put his elbows down on the bar and buried his face in his arms.

"Why, sure, it's been going on for a long time," he thought.

"The little tailor was smart, using me to hide him. The cops are smart – using me for a stool pigeon – everybody's smart." His mind opened up into great avenues of laughing faces. "Do you feel like robbing a bank? Do you get the itch? But you never killed anybody. Why didn't you kill somebody?" And then he looked up and called, "Heh, Eddie, there was a guy named Lazarus. Ever hear of him?"

"Anybody here heard of a guy named Lazarus?" Eddie said to his customers.

"Don't tell me, let me guess," a baby-faced blonde said sourly.

"They say he rose from the dead," Kip said.

"Sounds like a gag to me."

"What was his percentage at the gate?"

Two men and two girls came in and behind them came Jonesy and the girl who had been sitting with Kip.

"What's old Caley getting off his chest now? Let's see," someone said.

He felt crazy. He shouted, "I said I took a million dollars from banks. It's a lie! Do you hear? It's a dirty lie, you hear?" He got up, coming at them with his fists clenched. His face was wild. Pointing at Jonesy, he shouted, "It was two million –

that's a lie! It was four million, six million, ten million dollars."
They were all startled by his crazy, wild eyes. He kept running
his hand through his black hair. His head bobbed up and
down. Jenkins hurried in, standing at the door. The terrible
hurt in Kip's eyes scared him. Kip shouted like a circus barker,
"The merry-go-round is to the right, ladies and gentlemen,
but Mr. Jenkins will sell you tickets at the office. The ferris
wheel is upstairs." Picking up the pretzel bowl, he scattered the
pretzels the length of the bar, clamped it on his head and
shouted," The black boy with the silver hat – is there a lady
with a pin in the house? Step up lady and stick it in him, the
greatest freak in the history of show business." Everybody
started to laugh crazily.

"Kip's a card," somebody shouted.

Laughing, they crowded around him. Then he looked
frightened. "Go away, please, please," he begged them. But
they didn't understand. "Go on, please. What's the matter? Go
on," he said brokenly.

"Go on yourself," someone said.

The humiliation he had been seeking in a final destruction
of his dignity had come. His grin seemed to crack his face.
Lowering his head, he started to push his way out. In the hall
he went faster, on out to the street, sobbing. He wanted to
hide. A little group of people, arms linked, crowded the sidewalk, and he crossed over to the other side. He saw nothing.
He bumped into people drunkenly. How long he had been
walking he didn't know. When he looked around he was on
the bridge looking down at the freight cars and the moonlit
water with the giant shadows of factory chimneys. Across the
river were those large, lighted apartments; to the people in
them he had offered his aspiration that night he came home.

A plump drunk with a round, red, good-natured face,
came waddling along the bridge. When he saw Kip he came
over and said, "Mister, mister, how about a dime?" He tugged
at Kip's arm. Kip wheeled on him, and gave him a shove that

sent him sprawling on the road. On his knees the drunk looked up, shaking his head sorrowfully. "That's not a good thing to do, mister," he said.

"I hate your fat sloppy, good-natured face."

"There's nothing wrong with my face, mister."

"Go on, beat it," Kip said, and he leaned over the rail. The river flowed slowly down to the bay, rippling, then smooth, a little splash, then velvet dark. It had flowed like that when he was a kid, smooth and rippling in the fall, flooded in the spring. In the even, timeless flow there under the bridge the little ripples were like the voice of the priest talking about the city of God – good will, bad will, the thing he had been, the thing he was now and would be, all swept along to the lake like pieces of old furniture.

A freight train cried from the station yard, moaning on the night sky. He held the rail tight and waited as the train rolled under the trembling bridge. He leaned over eagerly; the black smoke rose up and engulfed him in the shriek of the whistle, in a belch of fire right underneath him.

Twenty-Two

HE WAS WALKING away, but the river still seemed to be in his head, flowing along, with him watching it, with everything levelled out in the flow like discarded rubbish. He thought he saw the Senator's old battered hat in the water. He seemed to be watching the flowing river, yet he knew he was going somewhere. When he got to Julie's place, looking up at the unlighted windows, he turned tense, hearing someone running. It was only a milkman rattling the bottles in the iron basket. Drops of rain fell. Climbing the stairs slowly, he rapped on the door. When there was no answer he put his ear down and listened.

"Who's there?" Julie called.

"Let me in," he said, pounding.

"I'm in bed."

"Open the door," he cried, pounding again.

"You'll have everybody in the hall," she said. When she opened the door and he went in, he leaned against it, watching her. She was in her nightdress. She looked very small and white and wondering.

"What's happened?" she said.

"I wanted to ask you something," he said. She waited while his eyes shifted around the room. A bunch of roses was in a jar on the little table at the end of the couch. The covers, thrown off the couch, showed the little hollow where she had lain.

"Where did you get those roses?" he said.

"Someone sent them to me."

"Who?"

"Someone sent them to the store."

He lifted the flowers out of the vase slowly, looking at them, someone else's flowers. Then he didn't know why he was holding them. They dropped out of his hand on the floor, while he watched her.

"What are you doing?"

"I didn't mean to," he muttered.

"You might have the decency to pick them up," she said, and she knelt down, gathering up the flowers, making them into a bunch again.

"Julie," he whispered.

She looked up fearfully, knowing he wasn't even thinking of the flowers.

"That first time at the hotel ..."

"I remember," she said, getting up, forgetting the flowers.

"Why did you come?"

"You gave me the shoes, don't you remember?"

"That's a lie," he said. "You found out who I was – you got excited – like the rest of them, didn't you?" He put his hands on her head, tilting it back, looking down at her face, really pleading with her desperately to deny what he said. "I remember the night I first held you – you trembled – your eyes shone, your cheeks were flushed."

"Don't hurt me."

"Tell me the truth."

"Yes, I was excited. You opened everything up – But there was more – courage and mystery, you were so gentle with me. Oh, darling – I think I loved you the first night at the lunch counter. Then to find you wanted things that had dignity ..."

"Yeah – dignity – the great dignity of jumping through hoops every night – the glory of the high diver," he mumbled.

"Oh, darling, what's going on in you," she said. He let her go. He had to grin at her.

"Jenkins tied a can to me," he said. "He wanted to turn me into a wrestler. People want to get rid of me."

"That's crazy – that's an awful lie," she said, looking up at him, mute and motionless with unbelief. "Why do they say it? Why do you feel like this?" There was the stillness of wonder between them.

"I don't know. I don't know," he said slowly. They kept looking at each other, both wondering that they were like this, touching the memory of that night when they had lain on the couch, talking of his dreams. "I been trying to get it straight," he said. He looked like a hurt, wondering child. "I guess I was blind," he said. "What made me like this? What blinded me? Years ago they couldn't have fooled me." He walked away from her, trying to break the stillness of their wonder. He turned, and looked at her expectantly, as if she might have thought of something. He was thinking of the years in the prison, the nights when he had gone over and over his life, putting a new price on everything. Then his hurt eyes were full of despair. The thing he had thought so big, this faith, the peace he had found, the innocence he had sought, had made him a clown.

"That's what did it," he whispered.

"What?"

"The thing I got hold of in prison ..."

"Yes."

"It blinded me – stopped me from seeing things."

"Oh, no, Kip, it gave you everything."

"It made me the town's whore."

"Then you don't believe in it any more?"

"I just see what it did to me," he said with that same child-like candor. "That's all."

"No, it's not it, it's not you, it's people that did it – they haven't got it," she said, pleading with him. The way he shook his head showed her how his faith had been destroyed. "No, no, no, oh, no," she said and she burst out crying. She threw herself down on the couch.

Standing over her, slow and puzzled, he said, "What's the matter? Did I hurt you?"

"Yes."

"How?"

"This thing – I wanted to keep it –" she said, her head in the pillow. She couldn't go on.

As he bent down and tried to turn her head to him, he was suddenly touched by the fear of being cut off from her forever. He knew she had built a new life on everything he had meant to her. "Sure, I hurt you, kid," he whispered. "I did it once before, remember? I guess I got to hurt people that love me. But I was getting the wool pulled off my eyes. That's a good thing, see?" When she didn't look up he stared at the white part in her black hair. He felt helpless; looking around he saw the flowers she had dropped on the floor. "They're mighty pretty little flowers. Here, Julie, here's your flowers," he said, picking them up carefully.

She was trying to smile at him. "It was the way you were feeling that was hurting me terribly," she said. "You don't feel like that, do you?" she pleaded. "Say you don't. Kip, you'll feel different. The priest has to be at the cathedral. Why don't you go and see him?"

But now he wanted to close his eyes and be in the darkness where everything would be different and not have to open his eyes on the light again. "I guess I'm through," he said, swaying. "I guess I'll go."

"Where?"

"To a hotel."

"No, it's too late," she said. "See, it's raining."

She got up and went to the window. And he stood with her watching the rain falling steadily. The pavements glistened like dark, glossy rivers with deep pillars of light on them from the street lamp reflections. "Stay here with me. Where else should you stay but here?" she said.

"I can't bring you any luck," he said.

"Just stay with me."

"I'm tired, terribly tired," he said. He sat down on the couch and watched her standing beside him in her nightdress. Then he lay down, his arm behind his head. His face was white and terribly tired. Kneeling down she began to take off his shoes. She had a little trouble with one of the knots. Then she lay down beside him and put her arm around him. Snuggling against him she turned out the light and rubbed her hand through his hair. She talked of going away and doing things in other places that could make them happy. The beating of her heart brought her close to him. But he felt very tired.

"I'll marry you if you want me to," she said quietly.

"You wouldn't want to marry me now!"

"Any time you say."

"Not now," he said. It was like looking over a city in shambles; it embittered him. Everything suddenly seemed to quicken. He sat up in the dark. "By God, I was the patsy, eh?"

"Kip …"

"So I have to take that, do I?" he said, getting off the couch and standing up. His quickening resentment seemed to give him back his life.

"People have been good to you."

"I haven't looked at anything straight for years," he said. "Sure, people like Butler were good to me, Butler's a saint, see. But what does that mean? He's against the field, he plays it his own way – a guy like him has to be against the field. If they catch up to him, they'll destroy him." He was standing in the dark, jerking the words out of him so rapidly he seemed to lose his breath. He began to stride up and down, his great shadow was thrown and broken and thrown and broken over her on the couch. "It doesn't matter how big a feeling anybody has for people, you got to keep outside them – if they catch up to you, you're done. They've got you by the tail, see? Butler feels it and runs away and hides in that jail, see! Me, the patsy! Looking popeyed at the Senator – big guys, big deals, big worlds, maybe there's a little money in it, the Senator says – all squawking about money! What a great big blockhead I was! Just floating around like a dead fish in a dirty pond." He banged his hands together savagely in a tremendous longing to destroy things. "So they're smart – they're hard guys – Jesus – I could buy and sell them at it." He laughed, jeering at them.

But she didn't answer him. He could make out the shape of her head on the white pillow and he knew somehow she was praying in the dark for him.

Twenty-Three

S HE HAD gone out when he got up. He made himself some
coffee. He started to dress and forgot, and found himself
moving around looking at her powder case, her comb and
mirror. Each thing as he handled it seemed to hold a little
more of her in the room.

He sat at the window looking across the street at the school
yard where hundreds of yelling children – little girls in white,
green and yellow dresses, and boys in sunsuits were flowing
into patterns in the sunlight.

He saw them coming down the street in the sunlight, Foley
leaning forward, carrying a bag, Kerrmann heavy and squat
beside him. Their faces were lifted up to the windows. They
were coming in like a couple of bill collectors. "What's the
matter? I don't owe them anything," he thought. Up the stairs
they came, clump, clump, clump, whispering outside the
door. He watched the door, his heart began to thump and for
some reason he thought of the prison and all the convicts who
hoped for a parole. He felt shaky as he got up. They came in
grinning.

"This is your bag, Kip," Foley said. "I was around at the
hotel and the boy at the desk told me you had left, and he said
Julie Evans phoned and said to send your things here – we
were coming this way." His voice was soft, patient and

indulgent. But he looked terribly happy as they sat down and took out their cigarette papers and tobacco, Foley started snickering to himself. The cigarette paper shook and he spilled tobacco. But he couldn't help it; he bent over and enjoyed a deep chuckle.

"What are you laughing at, you bastard?" Kip said. He was fascinated, as if Foley had some supernatural knowledge of what was to be the pattern of his life.

His face openly exultant now, Foley said, "Don't mind me. I got to laugh. I been saving it up. Was I right? Were you the two-headed dog? And he couldn't see it! The Queen of the May! Call me early, call me early for I'm to be Queen of the May." Every exultant little snicker from Foley was like a quick hot stab at him that cut off his breath. They were spreading the tobacco on the cigarette papers, still spilling flakes on the floor. For a moment Foley looked grave and sympathetic, then he started that terrible, happy chuckling again. "I hear you took the plug out last night," he said. "I wish I'd been there to see her blow." Taking out his handkerchief he wiped his face and glasses, and sighed.

"Pretty happy, eh?" Kip whispered.

"Why, sure," he said, "you great big slob."

"I don't feel like it, Joe," Kip said. But he felt he had to let this shining, glass-eyed little man gloat; and maybe if it came hard enough it would quicken him and free him.

Foley drew his chair a little closer. "Was I right? That's all I'm asking," he said. Kip could hardly bear the sight of his exultant face. "What the hell," Foley said. "You ought to be feeling like a million dollars. You've got rid of something." He couldn't help laughing again. Kip wanted to laugh with them, to laugh out loud, the room to be full of wild, crazy laughter; it would not come. Slowly he got up; his hands were tight on the arms of the chair; Foley and Kerrmann were suddenly alert. But he sighed and shook his head and sat down again.

"What do you say?" Foley said.

"About what?"

"Where do you figure you stand now?"

"Eh?"

"Why don't you get sore?"

"My God, look at him, he's not even sore," Kerrmann said.

"You great big soft slob," Foley said savagely, as if he hated Kip for sitting there all mixed up and dreaming. "Take the plug out. A big guy like you lets a lot of little no-account punks make a monkey on a string out of him." The words dug into that ache that was underneath Kip's stillness; he felt his heart jumping. "Yeah – where did it get you? Where does that stuff ever get you? Merde, merde, as the French say, and you know it, and if you don't know it they'll tell you. And, well – we figure they've told you, see?" But Kip still only sat there. With a sudden passionate vehemence, Foley said, "Every one of those mugs that was stuck on you a while ago works it for his own game. They've all got their hand in where it's soft, every one of them. And you – a chopping block you, see? A post, and if anybody's got a little extra virtue giving him a pain, he runs up and squirts it all over the post, you see?"

"Don't be so fancy," Kerrmann said impatiently. "Put it to him or don't."

"I'm doing it my own way, mister."

"Go ahead, get to it."

"First let me ask you one thing," Foley said, his voice soft and wheedling. "What have you got?"

"How do you mean?"

"What did they give you? Everything except anything you really wanted, or anything that had any responsibility attached to it. How much have you got out of it?"

"Not a cent."

"Right. But your rich friends – whatever happens they always get theirs, don't they?"

"And everything that goes with it," Kip said almost to himself. Suddenly it seemed to him that all the dignity and order he had wanted that the Senator and his friends had, came only from their money.

"Are you with us?" Foley said.

"I guess I haven't much choice."

Foley leaned back exultantly. "I knew you would, Kip. I knew all along you'd get wise to the set-up," he said. "I counted on you. Now listen," he said, drawing his chair a little closer. "Ike's got a car tucked away and he's changed the plates. There's a branch bank – the Standard, not twenty blocks away from here." Pausing, he said, "Are you following me?" He was still a bit afraid of that large untouchable stillness he felt in Kip. Kip nodded. "We've been checking on it all week," Foley said. "It's a soft touch, and we were wondering, on account of me and Ike not having much experience, and it not exactly being in our line ..." His voice broke; he looked at Kerrmann who nodded. "If you'd like to come in on it tomorrow or the next day...."

They seemed like ugly children, yet their voices sounded as good as most voices he could remember, the voices of the Senator, the Mayor, Judge Ford, other voices he heard night after night in the hotel. Neither their voices nor their faces in any way touched that little ring of warmth that held his feeling for Julie and his mother and the priest which was something held outside their world.

"You're absolutely right about it," he heard himself say. It would be so easy to get his coat and go with them. And he closed his eyes, dreaming.

When he opened his eyes their faces were close to him. He seemed to be terribly impressed with some discovery he had made in his dream. It seemed to fascinate him. "Listen, Foley," he said. "Maybe you've heard of the prodigal son."

"Who?"

"I figured you heard of almost everything."

"Sure, I know the guy you mean. What's the angle?"

"I just figured out what happened to him," he said, his voice a bit excited. "He sat around for months and months and it all wore off and he got fed up and bored and disgusted and maybe he stopped a few people on the street and said, 'Remember me, I'm the prodigal son.' Maybe they said, 'Oh, yeah, well I'm the king of Egypt. Out of my way big boy, I'm in a hurry,' and they pushed him off the sidewalk. So he got pretty sore and saw that the big feeling he had was just a shot in the arm for the folks of the town, then he cleared out, hating everybody, and back he went to the happy hunting ground."

"He's crazy," said Kerrmann.

"Shut up, you cluck. Let him ride. Go on, Kip," Foley said eagerly. But Kip suddenly looked distressed. He shouted, "What the hell are you going on like this for? I said, no – no – no ..." Surprised, Foley shook his head. "You didn't say no," he said.

"That's right, you didn't," Kerrmann said.

"I didn't."

"No. Did he?"

"No."

"It's absolutely cockeyed," he said. For years he had seemed so far beyond these two, and now, overnight, they thought he had become one of them again. "Look at the mess you made, look at the rug," he said. "I shouldn't have let you tramps in here. Pick up that tobacco," he said. He stood over them while they picked up the little flakes of tobacco around the legs of their chairs.

"Get going," he said. "It's getting late."

"How about tonight?"

"I'm seeing Julie for dinner."

"What time will you be back?"

"About eight."

"Maybe we'll wait for you," Joe said.

"Not around here, see?" he called as they went out.

Twenty-Four

A<small>T THE WINDOW</small> he watched them come out and stand on the sidewalk, looking up. While he was watching he saw Julie coming along the street. They turned and looked at her. She looked at them and started to walk faster, hurrying in. She came running up the stairs all out of breath. "Were those two in here?" she said.

"Just in for a minute."

"What for?"

"They brought me my bag from the hotel."

"What did they say?"

"Just talked," he said.

Looking around the room as if it had changed and she was a stranger there, she blurted out, "Why did they come?"

"I told you," he said. "They brought me my bag." Her fear and unhappiness touched his own doubt deeply. But he pulled away from it. "What are you getting at?" he shouted. "What are you implying? Am I responsible if they bring my bag around here?"

"No," she said, shaking her head.

"Then what's on your mind?"

"The sight of those thugs coming out of my place."

"Your place – your place, I haven't got a place now, have I?" he shouted. She looked surprised, then ashamed. "I guess they only grabbed a chance to come," she said. She kissed him. She stood in front of the mirror fussing with her print dress. "I'll have to be worrying about a fall outfit soon, and I'm tired of this straw hat already. I like felt hats ever so much better," she said. Giving her straw hat a careless tilt with her finger at the back of her neck, she shot it down over one eye and then she turned around and made a comical face at him. "I saw the most beautiful fall coat today, a sample," she said. "You'd have loved it! I tried it on and I felt so handsome in it."

"You'd make it look swell, kid," he said. "You could wrap a sheet around you and make it look like a million dollars. You ought to have fine clothes, Julie."

"I certainly ought to," she said.

Then he said in a slow, dreamy voice, "I could get you the best clothes in America."

"What's that?"

"Yeah, I could," he said, still dreaming and nodding his head. "No trouble at all." He was smiling and nodding to himself, not in the room with her.

Frightened, she came over to him and whispered, "What are you thinking of?"

"Why, nothing, nothing," he said, startled. "What's the matter?" He didn't know how he had come to say it. He had only been watching her; it had come out slowly, in a dreamy way. As she backed away from him, he shook his head, "Julie, Julie," he cried, pleading that she see he was just as astounded as she was.

"I don't want any clothes, do you hear that?" she said, coming close to him, shaking her finger at him, her face flushed.

"Sure, I hear."

"Don't you go worrying about clothes for me."

"I wasn't even worrying."

She went into the bedroom to powder her face and go out with him. For the first time she seemed scared. But it happened innocently. From the bedroom she called, "Ready,

Kip?" Yet he still sat there; it got a little darker in the room; his enormous surprise became a kind of terror.

They ate together in Angelo's, and they laughed and drank the red wine. But there was still the frightening break in the flow of their feeling for each other.

Twenty-Five

WHEN THEY went back to the apartment the old janitor told them Kip's brother had phoned. He had left a message for Kip: his mother was very sick and had only a little while to live.

"I guess Denis went round to the hotel," Kip said.

"Did you know she was so sick?"

"We knew she couldn't live. We knew it months ago," he said. But he seemed to be surprised as if he had just been given another push. "You go to the movies," he said. "I'll see you later."

Going downstairs he stopped and looked back, wondering if the ring of light that held her still held him. He crossed the road and took a drink from the fountain in the school yard, and then he went down the street.

When he was passing the corner cigar store Foley and Kerrmann, who had been watching, stepped out and got in step with him. "See you later. I'm in a hurry," he said. "My old lady's dying."

"Any harm in keeping you company?" Foley asked.

"I'm not out for a walk."

"You're not sore, are you?"

"I don't feel like clowning."

"Go on, call a cop," Foley mocked him.

"What's the percentage on just listening to us working out the proposition for you?" Kerrmann asked him.

But he was thinking of his mother, thinking maybe there was a right time for everyone to die, yet wishing very much she wouldn't die while he had nothing but sourness in his soul.

"You're stalling, Kip," Foley was saying. "Keep it up a few more months and everybody'll get wise to you and it's too late. What's the matter with tomorrow? If you're not coming in on it, we're going ahead anyway. But with you with us, why, it's as good as insurance – bank insurance," he snickered. "You're the last guy in the world they'd put the finger on." The coaxing voice murmured on. Sometimes Kip heard it clearly, sometimes it blurred as they tried to keep up with his great strides. Then he turned on them.

"My old lady's dying. Why don't you go to hell," he said. He swung his arm. They backed away. But when he started to cross the road by the barber shop they drew close together and whispered, not really convinced because he looked so distressed. They caught up to him when he was on the other side of the road.

"We'll stick around anyway. No harm in that," Foley said. They walked in step with him, their footfalls no longer separated from his own and he began to imagine that maybe it wasn't Foley walking beside him, it was just his own shadow, and Foley's whispering voice was his own voice saying the thing he knew was true. They passed the fire hall and the police station. The bridge stretched out ahead of them. They got to the street corner and that row of brick houses under one long roof, a very quiet little street.

"Keep on walking, you understand," he said.

"Have we got a date?" Foley said.

"Have we got a date?" he jeered. He shot out his hand and jerked the rim of Kerrmann's hat over his eyes. Laughing, he left them there under the light with Kerrmann cursing and pushing his hat up.

In the house, Denis was sitting with his arms spread out on the living-room table. His eyes were full of sadness. Beside him was a young priest with a pale, white, pointed face. They both got up slowly, staring at Kip as if he were drunk.

"How do you do, Father? How is she, Denis?"

"Kip, what is it?" Denis asked coming close to him.

"Eh?"

"What – what's the matter with you?"

"Me?" he said, frightened at the way they kept staring at him. Twisting the rim of his hat he grinned. His big dark face and his rolling eyes showed the terrible struggle going on in him. "Oh, God! Everybody feels it in me. Julie knows too," he thought. "I'm kind of broken up about the old lady," he said.

"I gave her a stimulant to keep her alive," Denis said. "Father Davidson has given her the last rites."

"Where's Tim?" he asked.

"The kid was crying. I told him to play outside on the street."

"I better see her," he said. And he went into the little bedroom where the wall light was dimmed by a scorching newspaper. His mother lay in a surprisingly small mound under the covers. Tip-toeing close to her, scared of the stillness, he whispered, "Mom, it's Kip. See, Mom, I came to see you yesterday but you were sleeping. Kip, Mom."

Her eyes opened, but she waited a long time as if waiting for the picture of his face to develop in her mind, and then she whispered, "I wanted to see you, son." He couldn't believe she was smiling, he couldn't believe that with death touching her she felt so much closer to him than she had felt at any time in his life; with that little smile and marvelous last flick of eagerness in her eyes she was offering him her gratitude. It was a moment she had waited for all her life. "You're good, son, yes, good, quite good, and I'm – I'm happy going like this. Don't worry. It's all right," she whispered.

He knelt down beside the bed, wanting to give her the last

faith he had held on to. "Take it along with you," he said brokenly. "Take it all along with you, everything that was good, you know, the things you counted on and kept going, the way you wanted me to be, take it along, it belongs to you. See, it's a fine peace. You can keep it. I want to give it to you."

"Say a prayer for me, son," she whispered.

"Sure."

"Now, son."

But he drew back, shaking his head, stuttering, as if she had asked him to mock her. "I don't know, I don't know," he mumbled. "God, God, nothing. Don't get me going on that." As she waited he felt that she, like everybody else, would see in his face the impulse to blow up everything. He ducked his head. He yearned to give her at least what she gave him, a last loyalty. "Holy Mary, Holy Mary, quite contrary," he mumbled. "How does your garden grow?" It got all mixed up. It didn't mean anything. He didn't want it to mean anything. Yet he wanted her to die peacefully.

As he got up she whispered, "Was it the Hail Mary?"

"Yeah, the Hail Mary," he said.

"I always loved the Hail Mary," she said. And he walked around to the other side of the bed, and then over to the window and pulled back the shade and looked out and saw Foley and Kerrmann waiting, leaning against a lamp-post. Their heads kept turning to each other, taking their time waiting forever.

"Who are you watching?" Denis asked.

"Me?"

"Who's out there?"

"Nobody, nobody," he said. But Denis looked uneasy.

"What's the matter?" Kip said, walking away from the window.

The priest was kneeling, repeating prayers for the dying. Kip stood beside him watching his lips moving rapidly in the prayer. The dim, shaded light mellowed the priest's young face. The voice murmured, then paused and the tongue came out and wetted the lips. Kip walked up and down excitedly till he couldn't stand the sound of the praying, and he went out in the hall. Turning, he looked at the priest's shoes, at the angle they made with the floor, the heels together, the toes apart at a broad angle. The soles were hardly worn. The priest, turning his head mechanically, following Kip as he walked up and down past the door. Then he seemed to feel Kip's excitement. "Please," he said getting up, "I'm trying to pray."

"Well, look, she's dying, isn't she?"

"That's why I'm praying."

"Maybe the sooner she dies the better for her?"

"Eh? I don't understand."

"No, you don't," Kip said. Then he was terribly apologetic. "I'm sorry, Father. See, I'm excited, the old lady was close to me. Are you from around here?"

"From this parish."

"Always here, never away?"

"Yes," he said. As he looked up at Kip his eyes brightened and he said softly, "I suppose you've been all over the country, city after city, always on the move, eh?" A kind of longing came into his voice. His head was tilted over on one side as if he were dreaming. Puzzled, Kip said, "You like big cities, eh?"

"I often think I'd like to see great stretches of country rolling by," he said. "But I like crowds. I like to see swarms of people. I'd like to get to New York. I'd like to see thousands of faces on the streets drifting by, but you've seen all that," he said. His rosary was hanging loosely in his hand.

"Gee, maybe he wants a little excitement, a change like I do," Kip thought. "That's terribly funny."

"Would you mind if I prayed now?" the priest asked.

"Please pray, Father," Kip said.

Then Denis came out to him and sighed and looked miserable. "I think she's gone now," he said.

While Kip looked down at his mother's face the few

moments of joy there might have been in her life when she was young and when she was first married seemed such a miserable compensation for so many defeats. Her jaw fell away loosely. He turned away, terribly hurt. He went over to the window and put his hand on the shade; they were still walking up and down, still looking at the window.

His mother's death was something won for them: it brought him closer to them. They kept turning, watching his shadow, pushing their thoughts at him, duelling with him. And he thought desperately, "It all adds up to this night here." Looking at his open-mouthed, dead-faced mother, he thought, "Old lady, I thought you were the big thing here, but I been ducking it, I brought it with me. They're outside. I'm glad you're gone, old lady, I only been half here with you. I've been walking up and down with those guys outside."

"What's the matter, Kip?" Denis asked suddenly.

"Nothing," he whispered. But he looked almost spellbound with fright. It all began to seem like a journey on a train; all the little points of interest flashed by in his head. The time when he got on the train in the prison, the hotel, a station where he changed and got on another train, still going, everything flicking past him, bright, exciting, the stop-off with the Judge. "Change here, change here, all aboard. I lost my ticket, mister. Where does this train go, mister? I'm on the wrong train, let me off, let me off, where's the next stop? I want a transfer. Why don't you stop it, blow the whistle, pull that bell." It had brought him here to his mother's death, the end of the line. He had to step out. They were there waiting for him.

"It's over," he said. "All over."

"Yes," Denis said. And even with their mother lying there dead it was hard breaking through this strange reticence and shyness that had always been between them. "I'll look after things," Denis said.

"Denis, stop staring at me," Kip whispered.

"You seem so excited."

"I've been upset. I've lost my job."

"That's a break for you," said Denis. He walked up and down, hesitant, a little shy, groping for some kind of an intimacy that had always eluded them. "Is mother's death and that job gone going to make much difference to your plans?" he asked.

"I don't know."

"If you need some money ..."

"Eh?"

"If you're thinking of going away."

"Where?"

"Come and see me, come tonight, will you Kip?"

"Sure – but I got a date right now," he said.

He waved to the priest who was picking up his little black bag. "So long," he said, and he went out.

When he didn't see Foley and Kerrmann he thought they had gone. But they were in the shadow beyond the next lamppost. They waited till he joined them. "Take it easy, jailbird, not so fast," Foley said good-naturedly.

"What?" he said. "Jailbird, jailbird, you keep calling me that." He felt in a frenzy to finish the struggle he had been carrying on with Foley while his mother was dying. He shot out his hand viciously, gripping Foley's shoulder. He drew the dark, smirking face close to him, jerked him off his feet, dumping him. All the resentment he had nursed against Foley's wisdom for ten years surged up, urging him to destroy him. His knee was on Foley's chest. The light was on Foley's screwed-up little face. The lips were pulled back; the brown, rotting lower teeth caught the light. He had his big hands on his throat. He kept choking him till the mouth gaped open wide. "Wise guy, wise guy," he muttered savagely, while Kerrmann jerked at his shoulders, pleading, "The cops'll be along. What's up? He's crazy."

He let go Foley's throat. "How did you like it?" he whispered. "You've had it coming to you for five years."

But the twisted grin was on Foley's puffed-up, bulging, glass-eyed face. "When are you coming back, jailbird?" he gasped.

"Eh?"

"You heard it. Let me up, you big lug."

Then Kip knew it was no good. His core of violence cracked up. After waiting years he had beaten up Foley; it had failed. He was kneeling on the sidewalk staring down at Foley's face. Even if he killed Foley, his violence would still fail, the voice would still be in him, the struggle still inside him. "Let me up," Foley said. Kip was shaking his head, his face full of wonder. It all had nothing to do with Foley. It was in himself; he had seen that years ago when he was alone.

"I was crazy, Joe," he said. "Why, you're an old pal. Look, my old lady just died, see? I liked her, but you say anything you want to. Talk your head off. It's all right with me, I tried to take it out on you, that's all. Look, how about some beer? I'll buy you some beer," and he helped Foley up. He dusted him off, fixed his hat for him and clamped it on his head.

Twenty-Six

W<small>HEN SHE</small> came out of the picture show and hurried home and put the key in the lock, Julie wanted Kip to forgive her for being frightened.

She heard voices coming from the kitchen. Hating herself, she listened. She heard Joe Foley's voice saying, "I'm telling you, you couldn't get a simpler set-up. Here's the manager's office and right here's the teller's cage. Tomorrow morning a red-headed girl will be on the books and a flossy kid with shiny hair in the cage. They're all kids. Why, you'd scare them stiff. We park here on Sherbourne, and come around to the front, see?"

As Julie took a step toward the kitchen and looked in the voice stopped. Foley and Kerrmann and Kip were sitting at the kitchen table. Foley had a pencil in his hand and was making a diagram on the shiny white tablecloth. Four empty beer bottles were on the table. Kip was slumped in his chair, listening, patient, unprotesting. When his eyes met hers she felt terribly lonely, then she couldn't understand why he didn't whirl on them savagely.

"It's your babe," Foley said. Kip got up slowly.

"We're having a drink. Come on and have one," Kip said.

"Not with them here," she said, backing away, desolate.

"They'll go, Julie. Come on."

"I'll wait till they go," she whispered. Looking at him help-lessly, she suddenly turned and rushed out. Halfway down the stairs she stopped, holding the banister tight and looking back. She took one slow step and then another, and then she could go no farther and she sat down on the steps and started to cry, seeing their three heads close together over the white table. "Oh, God! Don't let him listen, don't let him hear them. I love him. It's not him. It's not Kip. I don't know who it is," she moaned. She went out to the street and started to run down to the corner looking for a taxi. She started to half run along the street, her high heels tap, tap, tapping along the sidewalk, heading toward the cathedral. She got a pain in her side from running. Holding her hand against the pain, she ran till she saw the old brick cathedral with the illuminated cross shining in the dark sky. Up the cinder path she stumbled and tugged open the heavy door. She stood in the middle aisle staring at the red light over the altar in the silence of the empty church. "I'm crazy to think Father Butler would be sitting in here," she said. She went along the street to the cold, gray stone building with a light in the hall that looked ecclesiastical. When she rang the bell and a plump, white-headed housekeeper came to the door, she begged her, "Is Father Butler staying here? I've got to see him. Please, see."

"I think he's in bed, miss."

"Tell him it's Julie Evans. Please tell him. Hurry." Her wide-open, red-lipped mouth was sucking in the air. The woman began to look terribly worried herself. She led Julie into a little dull, brown-walled reception room with a few religious pic-tures. "I'll hurry, I'll hurry, but my leg's bad," the woman said. She went hobbling up the stairs.

"Dear Jesus, why doesn't she hurry? I prayed last night lying beside him and it seemed good, but it's happening. Why doesn't she hurry," she mumbled. Then she heard the fine sound of someone running down stairs, and Father Butler came in with a big grin on his freckled face. It was the most reassuring comforting human face she had ever seen.

"It's about Kip," Julie said. "I – " Then she stopped. No matter what was happening she couldn't bear being disloyal to Kip. "It was something I felt. That's all," she said weakly.

"Julie, hurry, hurry," he said harshly, grabbing her shoulder.

But she was appalled by the things she wanted to say and the words hardly came out of her. "They were planning a holdup – Foley and Kerrmann. I just heard a few words. It's a bank on Sherbourne – a bank with a red-head on the books." She told him what she had heard, how Kip had lost his job, how it had broken him. "I felt he would do something terrible. Stop him, please stop him. Oh, Father, I love him and you love him, too."

The priest's eyes looked so stricken Julie started crying, yet she kept looking at him, imploring him to help her. "It's been all wrong," the priest said bitterly, "all wrong from the beginning. They build up his pride in what he means to them and then they forget him and throw him away like an old glove."

"What are you going to do? You're not going to do anything to him, are you? You can't do that."

"He can come back to my house with me. He was paroled in my custody. He's out of a job, see?" he said.

Heartbroken, she whispered, "And he'll know I betrayed him. He'll know I put him where they'll watch him again. He'll never want to live if he can't be free. I love him – he won't see it."

"It's nothing like that, child," he said gently. He asked her to try and imagine how everybody in the city would feel if Kip's love turned to hate and he committed some crime of violence. People would remember how they had given him their faith and good will. They would harden themselves against all prisoners wanting a parole. "I love Kip, and you do too," he said. "But this mustn't happen. It touches something bigger than Kip. But we can work it out. You can be with him. Why can't you?"

"Can I, Father?"

"Of course you can."

"Could you fix it with him that he'd want me – we'd be together?"

"Why, of course I will."

"Then – I'd be glad," she said, "and maybe he wouldn't feel so bad."

On the way along the street they didn't speak; they seemed to be going separate ways, even when they climbed the stairs together.

In the kitchen there was still the heavy odor of tobacco and a layer of smoke high in the room. They stood together looking at the beer bottles on the end of the table and the three chairs. Julie was looking for the lines Foley had drawn on the table; there was just a smudge; a hand had rubbed them out. "See, it's rubbed out," she said. "Maybe they called it off – look, there's just a smudge. See what it may mean?"

"I know those two," he said. "Foley hates everything. If he could get Kip back with him he'd feel like a shepherd who had found a lost sheep."

"But the plan's rubbed out," she said. "Maybe Kip called it off. He'd be the one. Maybe it was all rubbed out easy like that. He'll be in," she said softly with a sudden ecstatic faith.

"We'll wait," he said. He sat down and took out his pipe.

She went to the window and looked down at the street. Every time anyone passed under the light she saw how much smaller and how much more insignificant he looked than Kip. In her troubled thoughts Kip grew larger and larger.

But she got very tired and lay down on the couch. The priest, too, became gradually pale and red-eyed. It began to seem as though they weren't just waiting for Kip. They were waiting for everything they had ever believed in and had ever hoped for. She became confused; she started to dream.

"It's no good," he said, waking her. "Supposing he doesn't come in at all? Supposing he stays with them?"

"What are you going to do?"

"There's only one thing to do."

"What?"

"I'm going to phone and have a policeman find Kip. Let them look for him. You see," he said slowly, not looking at her, "they can pick up Kip for hanging around with the two of them. I'll tell what Foley and Kerrmann are planning, and …"

"Who will you phone?"

"The Police Chief."

"What will he say?"

"I don't know. I'll tell him it's just a little worry I have and I want Kip returned to me."

"No, no," she cried. "No," she whispered. "No, no, you can't do that. You can't have them arrest Kip." She looked as if she longed to destroy him.

"Julie, poor girl," he said, his voice breaking. "What can I do? If we sit here and wait till morning, it's too late."

"Don't do anything. Oh, please, Father, don't you see? The plan on the table was rubbed out. It was a smudge," and she tried to smile, tried to make her voice soft and coaxing. "Don't have him arrested."

Father Butler rubbed his hands over his face. "What can I do?" he said weakly. "Tell me, girl, tell me. If he keeps away and we don't stop him, God help him. Look, child, I'll have to tell about the bank. They can stop that anyway."

"Why didn't I keep on trusting him? Have just a little more faith. What's the use of faith if it doesn't carry you right on?" It seemed to her that she had denied Kip's life and her own and everything she had ever wanted to believe in.

"Wasn't it your love and worry that brought you to me?" the priest asked her.

"I know, I know," she said, sobbing. "It's all my fault."

"All right," he said wearily. "It's not easy for me. It's the death of my own peace of mind forever. All right, will I do nothing?"

"I don't know – I – oh, I don't know," she cried. She threw herself on the couch. "Whatever happens I've betrayed him, that's death enough for me." But soon she was pleading again. "You love him, I know you do. Try and help us, try not to hurt him. Bring him back to me, bring him back safe loving me and not blaming me." It seemed terrible that they should be planning to have him arrested, waiting in this room where he had come that winter night, when he had met her in the restaurant.

"If I could have Kerrmann and Foley picked up maybe that would end it," he said slowly. "That would stop it. Maybe that's the way." He stroked her head gently. "I've never in my life betrayed any man," he said sadly. "But Foley and Kerrmann are habitual criminals. I knew them both in the penitentiary. If they're picked up, Kip won't go on, and then I'll have him, see?" He smiled. "I can't let them rob that bank. It would be on my conscience forever."

"Why, that's it, that's it," she cried. "Why don't you go? Why don't you hurry?"

"It's a hard thing to have to tell on any man," he said sadly. And he was very slow in going out.

She sat up listening. Sometimes she thought she heard a footstep in the hall; sometimes she seemed to be dreaming. Whenever she was wide awake she felt she had cheapened her life forever. She could think of nothing but Kip's face that first night when he followed her up the stairs.

Twenty-Seven

WHEN SHE next awoke there was a broad beam of sunlight streaming across the room. A bed cover had been thrown over her and tucked carefully around her; she felt warm and cozy. And then she heard a homely sound that had a magic beauty, the noise of a dish touching the stove in the kitchen. "Kip, Kip," she cried wildly, rushing into the kitchen.

He was standing beside the stove making a pot of coffee. His coat was over the back of one of the chairs. His black hair was all mussed up and he looked very tired.

"Kip," she whispered.

Hardly turning as he poured hot water in the coffee dripolator, he said casually, "What happened to you last night?"

"Where did you go, Kip?"

"Out after you," he said. "I couldn't find you. I had some things to worry me. I kept on going. I kept on going for hours. There were a lot of things I was trying to get straight and work out myself. I've made some mistakes. But I found out that the thing I got hold of belongs to me – it doesn't depend on anyone else."

She was watching his face for some sign of incredible violence and cunning. He only looked mild and tired as he listened to the hot water dripping through the coffee to the bowl below. She remembered how hard he was to defeat, how his eagerness and hopefulness always lifted him up. It brought him out of prison; it enabled him to go on after the Judge had humiliated him. She began to feel he was a bigger and stronger man than even she with her love had thought him to be.

"What time is it, Kip?"

"About nine, why? Want a cup of coffee?" he said. The mildness she saw in his face brought deep pain to her.

"Gee, Kip, I'm glad. Oh, I'm so glad."

"What are you glad about?"

"I don't know. I was talking to the priest –"

The dripolator in his right hand dropped and rolled around in a crazy circle spilling coffee on the floor. He came at her slowly, whispering, "Where did you go last night?" His wild hard eyes frightened her.

"Tell me."

"Just out."

"You went to the priest," he said. "You went to the priest, why did you go to the priest?" His fingers were bruising her shoulder. He gave her a little jerk that almost spun her off her feet. Somehow his amazement gave her a fresh and beautiful hope. "I thought you were going to get into trouble and I couldn't bear it if anything happened to you. I had to do something to stop it."

"What did you tell the priest?"

"I heard the three of you talking last night."

"About the stick up?"

"About the stick up," she whispered.

"What did he say?"

"He wanted to have it stopped, that's all."

"Stop me?"

"Have them picked up, that's all."

"The police," he said. "The police – no – you're kidding – you're kidding – the police pick me up. Me!" It was a humiliation he dared not think of. He shook his head. "You're kidding, you didn't do it, Julie," he whispered, begging her to tell him it wasn't true that the two people in the world he felt absolutely sure of no longer relied on him.

"He thought on account of you losing your job, you'd like to go down to his house," she said. Then she cried, "Oh, Kip, Kip, I'm sorry. I thought it was good."

"You've all been waiting, you and the priest and the rest. You and the priest with the rest. Me holding onto things for you. Christ! You and your love and him and his trust! Did he see the cops?"

"He – he phoned."

"What did he say?"

"He only wanted them to pick Kerrmann and Foley up, see? That's all, so they wouldn't get into trouble. He wouldn't have done it but he said he knew them – they were habitual criminals," she smiled, trying to make it a little thing.

"They didn't pick them up. I saw them this morning," he said. He seemed to be talking to himself, groping at something. "I went around to Foley's place early. They were sleeping there. I told them I had worked it out and they should count me out. But the cops haven't picked them up! What are they pulling? Something's cooking. Habitual criminals, eh! Yeah, that's it. Send them away for life." Then he swung around on her, hardly whispering, "See it! They'll let them go to the bank – they get them. They'll let them walk right into it – it's on me – it's my treat."

"No, not you," she pleaded.

"Why, you rotten little stool pigeon," he shouted at her. He shot out the flat of his hand, hitting her on the shoulder; she fell down. She dragged herself away from him, her arms held tight around her as if she was cold. She wept quietly and lay down on the couch. Her face was turned from him. She had only one longing, that somehow as he stood there mumbling to himself he would feel her shame and pity her a little.

"You made me a stool pigeon. Me! Turn me into bait for a police trap. You and the priest, my little pals ..." His laugh was a little crazy, like a sob. He started to shake her. She didn't cry out. She wanted him to hit her. She wanted to feel intense physical pain. Staring up at him, she pleaded with her eyes that he do this to her till it satisfied him.

But he whispered suddenly, "The time! The time. My God, what time is it?" And she had never seen such an expression of concern as she saw on his face as he grabbed his coat off the kitchen chair and ran out.

Twenty-Eight

As he ran out to the street it seemed to him that he had been the cause of the betrayal of two of his own people whom he had wanted to help in the beginning. The loyalty he still felt to all those left in the prison now seemed to include Foley and Kerrmann; they seemed much closer to him now than ever before.

Zigzagging out on the road like a crazy man he looked for a taxi. He started running down the street. There was a strong summer sun that morning. Children coming along the street on the way to school, turned to gape open-mouthed at him.

He got a taxi two blocks down, and it only took him five minutes to drive over to Foley's room over the Jewish delicatessen store. The taxi waited while he ran up the stairs and pounded on the door; but he knew that he didn't expect to find them there. He came leaping down the stairs to the sunlit street. He looked up and down helplessly. Then he went into the store and asked the little baldheaded Jew with the black moustaches if he had seen Foley go out and the storekeeper said he had seen him go out with a sawed-off fat fellow.

When he heard this he knew that the police would let them go to the bank and then trap them. Screwing his eyes up in the bright sunlight, the hot sweat drying on his head, he could think only of Judge Ford talking about justice. Judge Ford's voice seemed to be whispering to him that Foley and Kerrmann were simply ugly smudges on the bright pattern of the well-ordered city life that ought to be wiped off quickly.

"The Judge had a hand in this. He has a hand in everything that goes on," he thought. While he stood there he was struggling with the Judge again.

"Do you want me to wait?" the taxi driver called.

"Go over to Sherbourne and Queen," he said. He got in and sat on the edge of the seat, and looked out the window, telling the driver to go east slowly. He hoped he might see Foley and Kerrmann in the car.

When he saw the red stone bank building ahead he said, "Stop, let me out here." Jumping out he started to go along the street and the cabbie called, "Hey, don't I get paid?" Without turning, letting the cab come alongside, he shoved his hand in his pocket and pulled out the change. "Sure you get paid," he said. The cabbie thought he was drunk or doped.

He was a block away from the bank. As he crossed the intersecting street he looked down toward the lake. Far out the blue water sparkled in the morning sun. The bank ahead had just opened. It was just another quiet corner in the city that hardly needed a policeman. An old woman with a basket under her arm went into the bank. A car was parked in front of the drug store across the road. Three children came out of the drug store, laughing, with ice cream cones in their hands. One of the little girls with a big hair ribbon was in her bare feet.

It looked very peaceful in the city sunlight; but the peace was ending. He could feel them waiting. Slowly he loafed past the bank to the door of a stationery store. In his pocket was a little hand mirror and he took it out and shoved it in his package of cigarettes. About two inches of it stuck out. Then he stepped out on the sidewalk and lit a cigarette, shielding the mirror with his cupped hands. Nearly twenty paces behind him was a car with two big clean-shaven men in hard hats leaning out watching him. The sight of them sickened him.

Remembering that great power he used to have over people he wanted to jump out in the road and hold up his hands and cry out to passing people that this thing was wrong, that Foley and Kerrmann could easily have been picked up. He took a deep breath, getting ready to yell. But he suddenly felt terribly lonely. His breath came in a sob. What he thought should be done was no longer important to people.

Then he saw the car coming slowly down the street with Foley and Kerrmann in it. The sun was glinting on Foley's glasses. Kerrmann's hat was pulled down so low over his head his ears stuck out. They stopped the car, the engine running, and they leaned close together looking at the door of the bank. Whatever they were in themselves, as things spread out in a pattern for Kip that morning watching them, they seemed pitiful and helpless and not nearly as hard as the forces opposing them. They seemed to be his own people. His pulse began to pound. He went forward, feeling power and confidence, feeling on that sunlit street he was at last truly the mediator between the law and those who would break the law. He whistled, waved his hand. He started to run to them.

Kerrmann was pointing at him excitedly. But Foley, nearsighted, couldn't see him.

"Get going, quick," Kip said.

"Where did you come from?"

"For God's sake, step on it quick. It's a tip off – they've got you."

He had time to see the sawed-off shotgun half hidden by Kerrmann's coat and the gun Foley fingered in his pocket, then Kerrmann suddenly backed the car up and swerved it out on the road to turn. Kerrmann got the car turned, and Kip was feeling very happy, then there was a noise like the car backfiring. The noise came again, the windshield splintered, glass flew up and Kerrmann slumped down on his side while the car swerved crazily over the curb and cracked against a lamppost.

"Run, Kip," Foley yelled, and he jumped out of the car, his forearm shielding his head, his gun in his other hand. He fired wildly at the parked car where the first shooting had come from. As he lurched across the middle of the road he tried to look back and shoot. Stumbling he fell on his knees and his gun clattered on the road.

Helpless, Kip saw Foley kneeling in the sunlight, groping blindly for his gun. "Stop it," he yelled. Waving his huge arms wildly, he ran out to the middle of the road to Foley. "Stop it, stop it," he yelled. He was there in the sunlight, a forbidding, gigantic figure, trying to intervene – the mediator, the thing he had always wanted to be, only he was half sobbing. As Foley got up, the gun in his hand, the police were shooting again. Foley clamped both hands hard against his stomach, spinning on his heels, crumpling down, dying.

Kip grabbed Foley's gun. "Stop it, get back," he shouted; he was really crying out against all that dreadful irresponsibility which had spoiled things for him, and was now bringing about this brutal thing in the street that could have been prevented by the arrest of Foley last night. He loomed up, powerfully, threatening. But they kept shooting. It came like a hot stab at his shoulder; they had shot at him! In the name of peace and good order. "My God, me," he said. He looked all around with enormous, outraged surprise. Foley was sprawled on the road, his face twitching a little as he died. Foley's death seemed to come at him, a bluish evil death, mocking him; he had thought he could save him.

A cop with a big red excited face came rushing at him with his gun pointed. Kip swayed on his feet, his shoulder burning. He hated the irresponsible cop's excited face, which, as it came closer, blurred into a million such excited faces. He wanted to make one final, anarchistic rejection of the force he felt to be the only thing that held people together. Pointing the gun at the cop, he fired.

The cop stopped, stiffening a little, raising one knee, and

then he sat down slowly, clutching at his side. Kip looked at him, unbelieving. He got scared. He looked around and saw the car half on the sidewalk. Throwing his gun away, he ran over and jumped in beside Kerrmann, whose head was hanging loosely over the back of the seat. The engine raced as he shot the car back, and swerved around the corner, the tires whining on the pavement. For a few seconds doing this it had been almost peaceful; then they started to shoot. Car sirens were screeching. His own car was swerving all over the road with a flat tire.

When he had gone a couple of blocks he jumped out opposite a lane and he went running up the lane, his feet making loud scraping noises on the cinders. There was a row of backyard fences. He gripped the top of a fence and swung clear like a pole vaulter, his big body sailing gracefully and landing lightly on the other side. Keeping low, he was soon in the alley between the houses. He listened. The sound of shouting came up the lane. He was in a narrow alley with a green gate, and the gate would not open. "Where'll I go, where –" he kept gasping. His mouth was wide open, sucking in breath. In a frenzy he swung his body against the gate and broke the lock. But he had no plan. He wanted only to get over to the next block because along the alley he caught a glimpse of the quiet street under a beautiful horse chestnut tree. There was no sound out there; all the shouting came from the lane. He ran across the street under the tree and up another alley and was in a backyard with a little bit of green grass, clothes on a line, and a border of flowers around the grass.

When he took another step his shoulder was burning. It felt sticky. There were drops of blood along the alley. He still had no plan at all. "Jesus Christ," he sobbed. "There's no place, no place in the world." He looked around the little yard, and saw the open cellar window. He grew cunning. Bending low, half hidden by the clothes on the line, he headed for the back fence, leaving those drops of blood behind him. He put his hand

under his coat on his sticky shoulder. His hand was smeared
with blood and he rubbed it on the fence. Then he tore his
handkerchief, wiped blood on it and threw it as far as he could
over the fence on the green grass in the next yard. He looked at
the handkerchief, grinning with excitement. The rest of the
handkerchief he held against his wound and doubled back to
the open cellar window.

His feet, swinging through the window, hit the top of a coal
pile; a little coal slid slowly down the slope and he waited,
hardly breathing. Ducking his head in, he closed the window,
putting the catch on, and he was there in the suddenly cool,
musty-smelling darkness, his great weight moving him in a
slow, glacial slide down the coal slope. From upstairs came the
sound of a woman walking, and then calling to some children
and then hurrying into another room. If they had come down
then and found him crouched exhausted and bleeding on the
coal pile, he would have said, "I'm sorry, lady," and done nothing. He lay wedged in one corner, his side against the cool
cement, his fingers scraping lightly through the small, soft
Welsh coal. Then he began to draw the coal over his leg, scraping it softly from under his back and covering up his legs and
his body. Over his head to the right of him in the pile he
scraped a hole where he could shove his head if he had to and
jar the overhanging pile, and make it flow over him.

When they came running along the alley it sounded as if
there were fifty of them. Sirens were shrieking on every street
in the neighborhood. "See, see, he came along here, look at
those blood drops." Upstairs the woman ran to the back window right overhead and she yelled, "What's the matter?"
Somebody shouted, "Don't take any chances, shoot as soon as
you see the rat." They were down at the fence, quiet a moment,
then yelling excitedly and going over the fence and picking up
the handkerchief.

But it was the excited, frightened sounds of the woman and
the children upstairs that fascinated him; they seemed to have

heard something that stirred them deeply. The woman rushed to the phone and had a long, eager conversation with somebody. The radio was going, a low, smooth, rapid voice broadcasting the news; all over the city they were saying, "Yeah, he shot a cop." Looking at each other, hardly believing, then whispering, "Yeah, a cop, Kip Caley! No! Kip Caley! It's terrible, I feel terrible! I don't know why, I feel simply terrible. Say, wait a minute, maybe he didn't. Maybe it was somebody else. He wouldn't do it. Listen, I feel – I don't know how I feel, I guess I just feel something terrible." In homes all over the city, women were running around talking like the woman upstairs, each one feeling a deep, personal violation. He felt it and he sobbed. He lay in the dark, bleeding, his stiff, numb body half buried under the coal, with those sounds upstairs thinning out that whirling excitement that had kept his heart pumping.

"Yeah, I shot a cop, lady," he whispered to the moving feet upstairs. "Only it wasn't just like that. It wasn't like you think. It came out, I guess it had to come out. I guess it's been waiting for months to come out like the Judge said it would, only I'm glad it wasn't like he said it would be. Don't listen to him. He'll be there kidding you; he'll be in there talking about keeping law and order going, but come on down here and listen to me." He wanted to tell the woman he didn't just do it for Foley. Looking down at Foley's twitching face on the sunlit road he knew that Foley was evil. But it didn't matter. They were combing the city for him, the Judas; details of police spread out with a special hatred of him. Working men stopped cops on the street and asked anxiously if they could help. "Don't play around with him. Shoot to kill. I wish I had a gun myself. I'd like to get a shot at the bastard." The newspapers, the kids on the corners, would be shouting that Kip Caley had shot a cop. People grabbed the papers, read, lowered the papers, their hands trembling, looked worried and stood around in groups on the corners, too hurt to say much at first, their faith going, feeling the little bit of hope they had held shyly that men could change and want to be good fading out of their own lives. "Say, I'd forgotten about that guy, Caley! Why, they gave the guy the keys to the city; they gave him everything he wanted." That desolate, inarticulate wonder and sadness in the city people was heart-breaking. It was better for everybody when they recovered from the pain and were revolted. "I hope they get him quick and hang him. I'd like to take a shot at him myself. Let's go over and look around for him. I'll pick up a rock if I can get a shot at him." The newspapers were saying that was the right way to feel.

All his violence was gone; it failed as he knew it would fail the time he choked Foley. He was left with nothing to sustain him; his loneliness was greater than his terror. Swinging his head helplessly back and forth in the dark he sobbed; he couldn't even feel his body; he was terribly tired. Everything began to get darker. He lost consciousness.

When he awoke it was a little brighter in the coal cellar; the red summer sun was going down. A long beam came along the alley between the houses and touched the cellar window and made a little blotch of light on the cement wall. There was still the sound of footsteps overhead; only now the light, quick steps of the woman and the running patter of the children's feet joined by the firm, heavy, slower step of a man, going into the next room, returning, then stillness. Maybe the man home from a day's work was comfortable in his favorite chair with one of the kids crawling on his knee. These homely sounds aroused Kip. He listened, longing to hear more – the beautiful harmony of the unobtrusive life of a man in his own home with his own children. They were the sounds he had dreamed of hearing when he used to lie in his cell at night thinking of the kind of freedom he wanted in the city. A blotch of light shone on the wall in the dark; it rose a little higher and got brighter; it became almost a glowing red spot on the wall. Watching it, he suddenly felt that old, terrible, fumbling eagerness to keep the bit of light there. It and the sounds upstairs reminded him of Julie's room and how he had abused her and left her weeping. He began to long to tell her he did not die hating everything. With death sure for him, the memory of her was the bright, living part of him. He saw with great clarity how precious was the thing she had given him in their times together on the street, in the restaurants, at the races, and in each other's arms – the freedom he felt with her that night in the field by the stream. All his life some sudden surge of eagerness had quickened him in the dark moments. This was his last eagerness – he wanted to get to her and tell her he didn't do it because he hated everything, that he had not separated himself from the thing they had made between them. When he tried to move he couldn't feel anything. The bit of light moved up the wall across the unpainted boards of the ceiling; he watched it wildly, his mouth wide open. Then it was gone. It was dark again. But the dream was left still stirring him. His pulse was beating again. The pounding excitement came in his pulse. He could wait for hours.

When it was dark outside and the kitchen window threw a light outside on the grass, he began to crawl out of the coal very slowly, keeping flat on his belly, reaching up to the window ledge with his good arm, hauling himself up slowly. He choked a little from the coal dust. His blackened head came out. Above him was the lighted window, the path of light the length of the yard. The light, striking his head as he stood up, threw a great hulking shadow over the yard, and broke it across the back fence, and he swung out of the light, going down the side to the fence. He hauled himself over the fence and went through the yard and the alley onto the next street. No one was in sight. Ducking across the road, he went along another alley, over another back fence and into another street, getting closer and longing for home. Two blocks over, coming out of an alley, he found himself beside a woman who was sitting on the front stoop fanning herself. She rocked back in her chair and shot both her hands up, scared. "Oh, oh, Lord help me," she cried. "It's all right, lady," he said. But she knocked the chair over and ran in the house crying, "A great big Negro came out of the back yard."

A little way ahead was the big darkened school and the yard. Beyond the yard on the next street was Julie's place. He lurched across the yard, staggering and got into the shadow of the building. He felt almost elated. Creeping along in the shadow he got to the other side. There, spread out in front of him, was the yard where the kids played in the afternoon sunlight. There was the lighted garage, the fountain, people passing up and down the street slowly and Julie's lighted window. Summer moonlight shone in the school yard. The fountain trickled in the night air. Three boys on bicycles were leaning against it, talking, their young voices sounded loud.

His eagerness began to make him feel big and powerful again. "I can make it, sure I can make it," he whispered. Keeping his eyes on the lighted window, with all the times he had been with Julie enlarging him and strengthening him, he broke from the protecting shadow. He staggered across the yard. The boys at the fountain shouted. He stumbled past them in a frenzy of eagerness, hearing nothing. His breathing was labored and desperate like a tired dog's. A group of men at the corner were running at him. Everybody started shouting. Men jumped out of the cars. It was all whirling around in his head, but he went leaping through it. Stark still he stood, then he swayed. His back was burning. He stumbled as if he had been tripped. He seemed to have only one hip. The momentum of his drive, his great eagerness him going on to the door; it kept him crawling half way up the stairs. He was dragging himself up, sobbing for breath, his head lifted, everything tightening in him, trying desperately to reach the top before he lost consciousness.

Someone was running along the hall upstairs. He heard Julie scream. She was at the head of the stairs and behind her was the priest who had been waiting with her. Kip nodded eagerly to both of them, wanting to make something clear. "Kip! Kip! Oh, my God, Kip!" Julie screamed. His black, sweating face seemed to terrify her. All he could see was her face, her dark, thin, wistful-eyed face with the beautiful mouth that had always seemed to him to hold so much life.

"Julie!" he called. But they were firing from the door at him. "Julie!" He raised himself on his knees, then swayed like a big wounded bear, still nodding his head at her. "Julie!" he gasped, lifting his knees slowly. She screamed at the cops at the door, "Stop! Stop! You're murdering him!" When they kept on shooting, she screamed again. She came running down to him. She threw herself close to him to shelter him with her small body as they shot at him, her arms tight around him. Her arms seemed to loosen, then tighten convulsively. "Oh, Kip," she said. "Oh, Kip, darling." She seemed to be sitting beside him. There was no longer any shouting.

"See, I made it," he gasped.

But she choked. "I'm – I'm hurt," she whispered.

"Julie, kid –" he gasped, clawing at her shoulder. She sat stiff, her young white face childlike with wild surprise. She put her hand against her chest and bent over close to him. "Julie, I – I just wanted to tell you –"

"You don't need to tell me," she whispered.

"You had everything, Julie. We could have had everything."

"Oh, Kip – I – I brought you death."

"See – I wanted to tell you," he said, jerking the words out desperately. "You brought me life." Her hand locked on his arm; she couldn't speak. But she was trying to smile at him. He knew she was dying. But he had made a private peace with her; it held them together, it touched everything they had wanted. She fell over against him, the weight of her young body light and soft on him. He could feel their dream still in her. She was dying, so the dream for her got bigger and bigger. The dream got so big it was death for her. Then he fell back, lost consciousness and slid slowly down the stairs, giving himself again to the awed little crowd which jammed the hall behind the cops.

"I wonder if he's dead," a cop said, and he knelt beside him and put his hand on his heart. "No, he's not dead – good," he said. People at the door passed the word out to the crowd in the street that was getting bigger. They began to shout, "He's not dead, he's not dead – hurrah, they've got him."

But the priest was coming down the stairs, carrying Julie in his arms. His eyes were filled with tears. He laid her down gently beside Kip. Then he knelt and felt Kip's heart. Blessing himself, he began to pray for Kip and the repose of Julie's soul.

The cops and the people crowding the hall and door were scared of the sight of the dead girl. They were awed by the priest's detachment from them as he prayed. But outside they began to yell hysterically.

Somebody shouted, "Look at that priest. He's the guy that got him out."

"That's the priest."

"Praying for a rat like him in front of everybody."

"The cop killer."

"Don't let him die now."

"What right has a rat like him to be prayed for?"

The priest did not look up, but when he had finished praying he rose and took a few steps toward the door. He stood looking at the excited faces of those who were close to him. His face was hard. "What's the matter?" he cried out suddenly, his voice harsh. "You wanted a wonder man. You've got him, haven't you? He's here all right. What more do you want?"

Twenty-Nine

FOR THREE days he lay in the hospital and many policemen gave him blood transfusions. Sometimes he was conscious. There were moments when he heard voices that seemed far away.

"Can we keep him alive?" a voice asked eagerly.

"There's a chance."

"We've got to do it."

"He'll cheat us if he can," the voice of the police chief said. The shadowy figures kept going over to the window, looking down at the crowd in the street. All day the crowd was there. It got larger every night. They did nothing but look up at the lighted window where they knew he lay. Kip felt that crowd out there. Sometimes a voice said, "It's a wonder those people down there don't say something. They just keep staring up here. What are they waiting for? Can we throw him down to them?" It had become a desperate necessity not only for those people down there, but for everyone whose good will he had violated, that he be hanged. It was necessary that he be hanged in order that their pride and self-respect might be redeemed, that they might be cleansed of their humiliation, and that the pattern of law and order be finally imposed on him. They talked about the heart-broken Senator. The betrayal of his generous instinct was the betrayal of each one of them.

Everything Judge Ford stood for seemed to have been vindicated. Somebody shouted, "Hasn't he said anything? Doesn't he say a thing? The guy ought to be made to talk. Why are they letting him lie up there and say nothing?" They were outraged that he didn't pray that they forgive him.

While he lay there with his eyes closed, Police Chief Symonds, who had had his picture taken with Kip at the police benefit concert, bent over him. "Caley, can you hear me?" he shouted.

"Sure, he can hear you," a doctor said.

"Caley, why did you do it?"

But Kip's eyes remained closed, and there was no movement in the muscles of his face. "Caley, we're going to hang you if we have to put the gallows in an oxygen tent," the police chief muttered. "You're not going to cheat us of that, so you might as well talk." Straightening up, the chief said to the doctors, "If he's permitted to die – it's an outrage. Doctor, this is important to everybody, it's important to the fundamentally decent human instincts in everybody that this man should be legally hanged. If we miss out on him we're fooled again."

Then the young doctor whispered to the chief, "There's a chance to get him to talk."

"How?"

"His brother's outside."

"Brother? Has he got a brother? Oh, sure, I remember. Dr. Ritchie."

When Denis came in and stood beside the bed, looking at Kip's big, impassive white face, he seemed to feel a sudden lonely loyalty to him. He couldn't speak; he was remembering how Tim had come running to his office the night of the shooting, utterly desolate, crying, "Oh, gee, the kids say my Uncle Kip shot a cop! Why would Uncle Kip shoot a cop?"

"Go on, speak to him," the doctor said. "I'm sure he can hear you."

"Kip," Denis said, bending over him, "Kip, do you hear me? You should say something."

But Kip said nothing. While they were all staring down at him he seemed to smile a little; he had made his peace; he had made his peace with Julie and the things he knew were good that night on the stairs when they shot him.

He cheated them out of the hanging by dying alone that night without saying anything. His brother buried him from an undertaker's parlor at six o'clock in the morning when hardly anyone was on the street. The Bishop he had had lunch with ordered that he be buried in unconsecrated ground.

Afterword

BY MARGARET AVISON

If there were such a thing as a Celtic (anarchist) Jewish Roman Catholic humanist, Morley Callaghan is it. Am I saying he's a fence-sitter? No. I mean the terms in this way. Celtic: an (anarchistic) sensitivity to realities below the level of perception. Jewish: consistently spiritualizing the material and materializing the spiritual. Roman Catholic: firm of (private) faith, and absolutely steady-on about the value of every individual and the absurdity of the way we compare and prefer among our tiny selves. Humanist: courageous about faiths and approaches remote from his own private convictions. These characteristics are perceptible even in this early novel.

I remember the parole of the bank robber Red Ryan in the summer of 1935 and his death ten months later. Everybody was feverishly caught up in the story. It must have made Callaghan restless when people hastened afterwards to pack it all away, boxed in comfortable stereotypes. *More Joy in Heaven* reflects his private grappling with the whole business; he published the novel just a year later.

We grow accustomed to paperbacks suddenly appearing on the stands, purporting to cover events or persons while they are still in the headlines. This book did not ride the crest of a wave that way – although Callaghan had worked as a newspaperman and had studied law and was equipped to write that kind of journalism. He was a year late to capitalize on local interest, and reception was mainly in the United States, where the story's newsworthiness was scarcely a factor. Moreover, Callaghan had rather freely adapted the history to fit it around his own fictional parolee, Kip Caley. The novel remains as valid today as then when it was, almost, timely.

The facts may have gone stale a year later, but *More Joy in Heaven* was and remains fresh, the storytelling slowly gathering force towards events in the final chapters that rush the reader on, horrified and helpless, to the dénouement. And yet this novel cannot be read just for the story, for if it is, the reader will balk at the ambiguities, the seeming side-issues, and the style – all essential to the book's meaning. The novelist betrays his own deep concerns, and these certainly antedated the Ryan events.

There is proof. In his autobiographical *That Summer in Paris,* Morley Callaghan tells of meeting on shipboard, in the 1920s, a Canadian prison chaplain. They became friends, and Morley and his wife Loretto made a point of spending more time with him when his travels brought him back to Paris on his way home. In these conversations a groundwork was laid, years before the novel, for pondering the human spirit's response to crime and punishment, and the meaning of a fresh start.

Such general terms are sorely un-Callaghan; I apologize for them. In *That Summer in Paris,* Callaghan reports that he liked to wander the streets, looking at everything, filling his reservoirs with this object, that face, those gestures. "Why couldn't all people have the eyes and the heart that would give them this acceptance of reality?" he cried. Being committed to regard the uniqueness of every person, he did not present Kip as a psychologist's case or as a victim of class oppression. Callaghan was aware of such approaches, and rejected them. Kip's brother does see in class terms. "Why stick around here," he asks Kip, "and let that big tycoon, Senator Maclean and his friends have a field day with you? Maybe he's generous, but he's irresponsible. They're all irresponsible." But Kip can only say, "I guess we both try and do it the way we see it." Callaghan's stamp is on those words.

Publicity pressures, central in this story, have not changed with time; the spotlight can still make someone an instant celebrity, and as quickly move on. Kip had been singled out very early. Taller and brawnier than others, with more intelligence than most, he had always had a feeling of being special. "I never wanted to work with anybody – that's where I jumped the tracks," he muses in prison. Isolation led to prison, but there he met Father Butler, a catalyst for simple friendliness in that unlikely community. It was a new beginning. "Getting close to other men and getting out of himself did it," says Father Butler.

Kip's plan is to live quietly with ordinary people on his release. He does get out. And he finds himself with people, but as a special person again, in the limelight, pushed into unhealthy excitement from every quarter. Poor elated Kip misreads the situation. He wants to help people to be hopeful. He wants to mediate between prisoners and the people on the outside. One newsman suggests that he try for a seat on the parole board. One prominent sponsor is rash and inattentive enough to let him persist in this dream. Of course his idealistic plan is thwarted, his glamour fades for the paying public, and his well-off sponsors have nothing then to suggest except a safe small-time scam. Kip refuses to be compromised that way. There are left to him only four people: two questionable friends from his past; and the two people he loves, Julie and Father Butler.

The novel's plot makes sense. People who respond to Kip on his release and influence his choices and his aspirations become part of the mesh of circumstances that snare him. The "tragic flaw" is not in them or in "society" or in Kip, it is in all of them.

This is a man's version of a man's world; later on – by *A Passion in Rome* – much had changed in Callaghan's approach. In *More Joy in Heaven,* however, the laconic way the men talk with each other supports Callaghan's impatient drive in his narrative to convey the particular nakedly, not to talk about it. Callaghan seldom lets his own voice be heard. The characters speak, and think, in their own ways. Descriptions are usually offhand: a loosened tie, slushy streets, a "pudgy pompous man." But when Callaghan does speak the sound is distinctive, as, for example, right at the beginning of the book: "The country seemed to rise up all around him in the snow, dawn light and loneliness"; and towards the end, through Kip's eyes but in Callaghan's voice:

> As he crossed the intersecting street he looked down toward the lake. Far out the blue water sparkled in the morning sun.... An old woman with a basket under her arm went into the bank. A car was parked in front of the drug store across the road.... It looked very peaceful in the city sunlight; but the peace was ending. He could feel them waiting.

Callaghan commands language very confidently. Surely, then, he is deliberate when he re-uses key words, for example, "excited." The Senator and Kip both like "excitement," even though Kip finally has an appalled glimpse that this "excitability" comes out of a core of violence. More obtrusive is the word "eager" in its various forms – a rough count shows twenty-eight instances in twenty-nine chapters, and the chapters are very short. Why? Perhaps the quality that Callaghan wanted in style – directness, transparency – was a quality he wanted in people: candour is a primary value for him. Whatever action or speech rises "eagerly," right from a person's nature just as he is, has impetus for good – or ill. In this novel there is a dynamic in "eagerness," and sometimes it is dangerous. Callaghan lets the word keep on radiating. Perhaps he figured that if it bothered us enough we would ask some questions useful to our reading of this book.

Does Callaghan present Kip as the "good guy" (as the "sinner who repents," in the words of Luke 15:7, who occasions "more joy in heaven")? Not unequivocally. The Judge declares sourly that there is "more joy on earth than there is in heaven" over this ex-con. And Kip gets muddled trying to apply to himself the parable of the prodigal son. When a crush of partygoers swarms around him for a piece of his time and attention, Father Butler is worried. Kip sees no harm in it: "Listen, what would you have thought of the prodigal son if he had come home, and found his old man and his family had got a big feast ready and invited all the neighbors in and they were all getting ready for a swell time, and the son takes one look at them and refuses to sit down on account of them wanting to make a fuss over him?... They have to call it all off ... because he's feeling sour. A killjoy." Father Butler responds wryly: "That's quite an idea. Maybe the prodigal son had a job going from feast to feast till the end of his days." Only in a turmoil of indecision months later does Kip remember those words – to use them savagely against himself. He has understood.

Why, in the mischievous novel *A Fine and Private Place*, did Callaghan's alter ego ignore this novel and pick out the earlier one, *Such Is My Beloved*, to praise? I have a notion that he passed over this book in hindsight, because he was uneasy about an unobjective intensity he sensed he had brought to the writing of it.

More Joy in Heaven is about "outcasts and right-thinking people" – Kip's terms – and about a person wanting to bridge the gap between those "two worlds" even though it is pulling him apart. Kip's "two worlds" are very different from those of Callaghan, who never saw in black and white.

Yet Callaghan shared Kip's eagerness to test his values in the crucible of everyday reality. He too struggled to communicate across the chasm that separates any "two worlds." For example, old Ontario in the thirties was massively Protestant and, to some degree, anti-Catholic; even the more sensible on either side were aware of the cultural differences. Yet it was a familiar tension, one the Callaghans seem to have accepted with aplomb when they decided to settle down in Canada. *That Summer in Paris* comes to an abrupt end with Morley and Loretto realizing together that they would leave Paris – for Depression-time Toronto. The Left Bank had been wonderful: Callaghan's fame as a short-story writer, early established in the United States, had preceded him to Paris where he was in the literary limelight, one of a select (American) group. But a person's place of origin retains a strong hold even when one had been glad to escape from it. Kip's words to Julie are pertinent: "A guy feels a little sour, and wants to pull away from everybody.... He goes off on his own.... But he's got to come back."

True, Callaghan kept strict boundaries between his private life and his public work. But, looking back on *More Joy in Heaven,* he might have suspected that this time he had let preoccupations of his own get into his fiction.

There is appalling venom in one of the final scenes in this novel: "Look at that priest. He's the guy that got him out." "That's the priest." "Praying for a rat like him in front of everybody." I wish the ugly prejudice had been an exaggeration, but the tone is true to that time. Callaghan is simply recording it. He was too aware of ambiguities to write polemically. For example, he has the Bishop acknowledge that "Of course, as a Christian he *had to believe it possible* in a man to change the pattern of his life, but he *knew* it hardly ever happened." Whereas Father Butler says, "The trouble is there's probably more public curiosity about him since he *became a good man* than there was when he *was* a notorious bank robber, and it worries me." (The italics are mine.) The disparity here is between defensive common sense and creative trust. In yet another section, the sketch of a short story about "the little tailor," moral law clashes with civil law, and the ex-con and the priest alike know the torment of facing the choice. Later, Kip's girlfriend and the priest are both in the same anguish, weighing responsibilities of the heart against those of principle. She cries out: "Whatever happens I've betrayed him, that's death enough for me."

Perhaps Callaghan did not write *More Joy in Heaven* out of first-hand wrestling with basic values, but certainly we must be willing to face something of the kind ourselves to give it a proper reading. The novel leaves us with the stricken suspicion that if we ever think we can balance things out neatly and put them away, we are kidding ourselves. The Ryan story has been transmuted; the book that may have taken colour from Morley Callaghan's embattled convictions stands ready to engage anyone else's still.

BY MORLEY CALLAGHAN

AUTOBIOGRAPHY
*That Summer in Paris: Memories of Tangled Friendships
with Hemingway, Fitzgerald, and Some Others* (1963)

DRAMA
Season of the Witch (1976)

FICTION
Strange Fugitive (1928)
A Native Argosy (1929)
It's Never Over (1930)
No Man's Meat (1931)
A Broken Journey (1932)
Such Is My Beloved (1934)
They Shall Inherit the Earth (1935)
Now That April's Here and Other Stories (1936)
More Joy in Heaven (1937)
The Varsity Story (1948)
The Loved and the Lost (1951)
Morley Callaghan's Stories (1959)
The Many Colored Coat (1960)
A Passion in Rome (1961)
A Fine and Private Place (1975)
Close to the Sun Again (1977)

New Canadian Library
The Best of Canadian Writing

Morley Callaghan

More Joy in Heaven
Afterword by Margaret Avison

Such Is My Beloved
Afterword by Milton Wilson

*They Shall Inherit
the Earth*
Afterword by Ray Ellenwood

Raymond Knister

White Narcissus
Afterword by Morley Callaghan

NCL – A Series Worth Collecting